HER VENGEFUL EMBRACE

AN ISLAND OF YS NOVEL

KATEE ROBERT

To all the fans of Death out there.

ALSO BY KATEE ROBERT

The Island of Ys
Book 1: His Forbidden Desire
Book 2: Her Rival's Touch
Book 3: His Tormented Heart
Book 4: Her Vengeful Embrace

The Wicked Villains Series
Book 1: Desperate Measures
Book 2: Learn My Lesson
Book 3: A Worthy Opponent
Book 4: The Beast

The Thalanian Dynasty Series (MMF)
Book 1: Theirs for the Night
Book 2: Forever Theirs
Book 3: Theirs Ever After
Book 4: Their Second Chance

The Kings Series
Book 1: The Last King
Book 2: The Fearless King

The Hidden Sins Series
Book 1: The Devil's Daughter
Book 2: The Hunting Grounds
Book 3: The Surviving Girls

Book 1: Mistaken by Fate

Book 2: Betting on Fate

Book 3: Protecting Fate

Come Undone Series

Book 1: Wrong Bed, Right Guy

Book 2: Chasing Mrs. Right

Book 3: Two Wrongs, One Right

Book 3.5: Seducing Mr. Right

Other Books

Seducing the Bridesmaid

Meeting His Match

Prom Queen

The Siren's Curse

CONTENT WARNING

This book contains characters with a history of childhood abuse (that is *not* described in graphic detail in the story).

CHAPTER 1

The Warren was nothing like Amarante expected.

She stepped out of the car she'd rented upon arriving in Switzerland and looked at the massive building sprawled into the nooks and crannies of the mountainside. Intelligence said half the floor plan was actually carved into the mountain itself, but she'd still expected something... subtler. It looked like a lodge or resort or something designed to draw people in, which was the last thing the Warren aimed to do. Or, rather, it had no interest in the kind of tourist activity the other resorts in this area catered to.

With two checkpoints and forbidding-looking, well-trained guards, there was little danger of said tourists wandering in at an inopportune time. Rich people liked what they liked, even the criminals. *Especially* the criminals. It stood to reason that nothing but the best, most blatantly expensive, would do.

A bellman appeared to unload her luggage, but Amarante's focus fell onto the white man striding out the main doors in her direction. Even knowing what little there was to know about Nicholai Krylov, it still surprised her to see how young he looked in person. He was a few years younger than her thirty-two, and while he hardly had a baby face, his large green eyes seemed almost innocent. Or maybe it was his full mouth. She didn't know, but she didn't trust it. Not when she knew in gory detail exactly what happened to those who crossed this man.

Certainly not when Amarante would number among them before the week was out.

Strange to shake the hand of the man who would soon attempt to kill her, but these were strange times. She didn't bother to smile or weaken her grip, and neither did he. It made her like him a little.

Nicholai nodded at her luggage. "My man will see to it."

No doubt after ensuring she wasn't hauling in weapons. The Warren was a designated neutral space and Nicholai and his people enforced that to the point of death. Very few dared break the rules, because he made an example of anyone who crossed that line.

She couldn't think too closely about that now. Amarante was here for one reason and one reason only. To close the circle of suffering her father began when he sent his only children to Camp Bueller at the tender ages of five and seven. He hadn't expected them to survive. Surely he hadn't expected them to flourish as they had, or for them to hunt *him* down.

"This way."

She fell into step next to Nicholai easily. He didn't bother to check his longer stride for her, which only added to her reluctant liking of him. Nicholai wasn't a man who would pull his punches, and she respected that, even if they were destined to be at odds.

He led them through the entrance of the Warren. It looked much like any other high-end resort, including the one Amarante owned with her three siblings, though the decorations all reflected the Swiss location. Strong lines. Exposed dark wood beams and gleaming floors. It was a little cold and impersonal, but she liked it.

Nicholai didn't speak until they'd left the main room behind and headed through the wide halls deeper into the building. "The summit with Zhao Fai begins at eight tomorrow. The schedule will be in your room."

That set her back. "Schedule."

"Yes, schedule." He turned left at a T in the hall. "There are several meals beyond the meetings themselves where he would like your attendance."

She had to fight not to clench her jaw, to allow the news to roll over her and away. Forcing her to adhere to a schedule was a power play, and she would have organized something similar if she'd put this together. Her father wanted her dancing to his tune.

Very well.

She'd dance to his tune. Right up until the moment when she slipped in close and gutted him.

"Ms. Death." Nicholai's tone didn't change when he used the name she went by to everyone but her family, but the small hairs on the back of her neck rose in response all the same. He stopped and looked at her. Had she thought his green eyes made him look young? Hardly. They were eerie, the kind of eyes one expected to see peering out at them from the shadows, the only warning before a predator appeared and ripped their throat out.

She kept her expression cool and unaffected. "Nicholai."

"I don't care whether you make polite with him or not. That's not my problem. The only thing I *do* care about is preserving the sanctity of the Warren. You will not move against him or his people while you're under this roof, nor while you're traveling back to your home. Beyond that, carry on with your protracted vengeance to your heart's delight, but if you violate the rules, I will string you up for everyone to see." He slid his hands into his pockets, as relaxed as when he'd welcomed her ten minutes ago. "You have a reputation. I respect that. But while you're on this property, I am the god everyone pays fealty to. Even you."

She raised her brows. "A god, Nicholai? Someone is reaching high."

"There's no higher than me. Not here. Agree and stay. If you can't abide by the rules, I'll have the driver take you back to the airport."

She had no intention of abiding by the rules, but Amarante knew better than to admit as much. Nicholai wouldn't strike until she stepped out of line, so she had to ensure that when she did, it would count. She didn't bother to smile. He'd see right through it. "I agree."

He studied her for a long moment as if delving deeper into the two words for the truth beneath. He would find nothing. Amarante had learned to keep secrets far too young, when her and Ryu's survival depended on it. She kept her brother safe with her ability to hide what she was thinking, and when Luca and Kenzie had come along, she kept them safe, too.

Finally, he nodded. "There are several restaurants on the property, and we are able to accommodate if what you're craving isn't on the menu."

Layers beneath layers there. The Warren functioned much like the Island of Ys, though for very different purposes. Both kept their patrons content by providing a number of services both mundane and unorthodox. The Warren did it to keep people happy and tempers down. Amarante's resort did it in order to cast a wide net for people who had useful information. "I'll take that into consideration."

Nicholai made several more turns. Amarante had a superior internal compass under normal circumstances, but they'd long since passed into the depths of the mountain and the twisting hallways played with her senses. She was sixty percent sure she could find her way back to the main entrance from here, but she preferred better odds when playing with her survival.

Her siblings would say she was suicidal for attending this summit with the intention of murdering her father. They were wrong. As long as she drew breath and her heart pumped blood through her veins, she had a chance to survive. She wouldn't resign herself to the sweet sleep of death until the Reaper himself tore her soul from her body. No matter how insurmountable the odds seemed, there was always a new angle to consider.

She couldn't bribe Nicholai. His very power was grounded in being neutral. The second he faltered in that, the people who moved through their world would tear him to pieces—if the former leader of the Warren didn't do it first. For that same reason, she couldn't threaten or bully him into letting her have her way. He was a clean slate as far as blackmail went. If Ryu couldn't find dirt to use against him, it didn't exist.

Still, there had to be another way.

They turned another corner and then another. Amarante opened her mouth to ask him why he was taking them in circles when a figure walked out of a door down the hall. Even knowing that she'd see him here, having Tristan appear in front of her like a phantom still shocked her enough that she almost missed a step.

He looked... good. Very, very good. The years since she'd seen him last had propelled him from a nearly-starving teenager to a man who was at home in his skin. His blond hair was cut short and serviceable and he moved in a smooth way she recognized. Her brother Luca moved like that. He'd gone from brawling for his life in Camp Bueller to more structured training once they had the safety to make that happen. Tristan didn't have the same background as Luca, but he had the same skillset.

He watched them approach, his gray eyes holding nothing even as his mouth curved into a little smile. "Amarante." He said her name like he was tasting it, tasting *her*.

You don't get to call me that. She managed to keep the response behind a slow smile of her own. "Tristan." She didn't comment on the fact he'd tried to kidnap her younger brother less than twenty-four hours ago. It wouldn't rile him, and it would only put her at a disadvantage to comment on it.

Nicholai gave him a look. "Where is your escort, Tristan?"

"Around." He shrugged massive shoulders. His smile widened, inviting them in on a joke. "I felt like exploring."

"The rules—"

"I'm not causing mischief, Nic. Just needed some time to myself." Tristan laughed. "Take that stick out of your ass and live a little."

Nicholai rolled his eyes. "You're nothing but trouble."

Alarm bells pealed through her head. Some of the coldness that coated Nicholai thawed in Tristan's presence, which indicated that they were... friends? The allowance of a shortened name only reinforced that truth, along with the fact that Nicholai wasn't immediately calling for his missing employee to resume escort duties. It all added up to give Tristan what equated to a home court advantage. He might not get away with breaking the most sacred rules, but he'd be able to move about without a chaperone to ensure good behavior.

She drew icy professionalism around her like a cloak and raised a single eyebrow. "Are we done here, *Nic?*"

"By all means." He motioned her forward with a careless wave of his hand. Right in the direction of Tristan.

She had a moment of wondering if this was an ambush of some sort. Just because every single piece of evidence supported the theory that Nicholai was incorruptible didn't mean it was the truth. After all, Amarante excelled at finding pressure points and using them to get people to act in her best interests. Tristan was just as good as she was. Better, in some cases.

She didn't lift her chin or throw her shoulders back. She didn't do anything but walk toward him in measured steps.

He raked her with his gaze, a heated slide she could feel through her clothing. "Nice suit."

"Wish I could say the same." He'd left his jacket some-where, unbuttoned the top few buttons of his pale gray shirt, and rolled up his sleeves. It should have made him look relaxed and at ease. Even sloppy. Instead, he looked ready to get into trouble. Whether that trouble was brawling or women, she couldn't begin to say.

She refused to contemplate either.

He grinned at her, all wicked charm and dangerous amusement. "Missed you, Te."

"Don't call me that." She regretted the words as soon as they flew from her mouth. Point to Tristan for taking a grand total of two minutes to get under her skin. She forced her hands to relax, forced the tension from her shoulders, forced herself not to telegraph her desire to rake her nails across his ruggedly handsome face and scar him the same way he scarred her in places no eye could discern.

His grin widened, acknowledging her slip of control. Amarante tensed. A smile from this man was like a predator showing its claws. She didn't *think* he'd attack her right here in front of Nicholai, but the days when Amarante thought she could anticipate Tristan's actions had passed right around the time he betrayed her.

Nicholai cleared his throat. "That's enough of that." He stepped between them. Even though he was several inches shorter and built much leaner than Tristan, he made an effective wall. Whatever passed between them in that moment was enough for Tristan to back up with his hands held up, his easy smile never faltering.

"Be seeing you, Te."

She was stone. She would *not* react again. Doing so the first time had given him a weapon to use against her. Now, he'd say the nickname that only her family used over and over again, digging beneath her skin in an attempt to make her lose control. She wouldn't. She couldn't afford to. Fifteen years of searching, of building a small empire in her quest for justice, and she'd never been this close before.

Nicholai waited until Tristan rounded the corner and moved out of sight to turn back to her. "I owe you an apology."

She slipped her hands into the pockets of her slacks, intentionally mirroring his relaxed pose. "Are you in a habit of making exceptions to the Warren's rules for your friends?"

He didn't exactly wince, but his jaw tightened. "It won't happen again."

He wouldn't give her the same leeway he gave her enemy, but still better to start this process off with Nicholai feeling a bit off-center over this minor screw up. Amarante gave him a sharp smile. "Forgive me if my trust is somewhat damaged."

Now the muscle definition in his jaw was clearly defined. "I suppose you have an idea on how I can make amends."

"I do." She smiled. "I'd like to see the meeting rooms now."

Nicholai sighed. "You know part of smoothing the way through negotiations is ensuring everyone comes in on the same playing field here. That means no advance walk-throughs."

"Nicholai." She drew his name out. "You know very well that the other players have an advantage. They set the schedule and apparently members of their party are able to walk the hallways unmonitored. If anything, showing me an advance look at the meeting rooms will remedy an *uneven* playing field."

He looked like he wanted to argue, but finally shook his head. "I knew I shouldn't have agreed to this. You all are going to be the biggest pain in the ass while you're here."

"Undoubtedly."

"Fine. You can see the meeting rooms briefly before we reach your room, where you will stay until someone is sent to fetch you in the morning."

That most definitely wasn't going to happen, but she still nodded. "Of course."

He gave her another long look and shook his head again. "Come along."

CHAPTER 2

*T*ristan followed Amarante and Nic at a distance as they moved through the halls to the meeting rooms set up for the summit tomorrow. *Summit.* He shook his head. A pretentious-ass word for a meeting that he still wasn't sure what Zhao intended to accomplish. If he wanted to take Amarante the same way he'd instructed Tristan to take her brother, Ryu, a few days ago, there were better and less expensive ways to go about it.

No matter how secure they thought the Island of Ys— their little trio of islands off the coast of Africa—was, nothing was too secure for *him* to get through.

He shadowed their steps, listening to the cadence of Amarante's voice as she questioned Nic about the set-up. She was so fucking cold, and though she was only a handful of feet away, she might as well have been on the moon for the distance she put into her careful selection of words.

She didn't used to be like that.

He banished the thought. It didn't matter that he and Amarante had a history of sorts. It was as dead and buried as every other part of his past. He waited for Amarante and Nic to enter an elevator before he turned back the way he'd come. Once she reached her floor, there was no getting to her easily. The Warren's elevators were locked far more securely than any civilian hotel. In addition to the requirement of a hand scan to reach the correct level, there were also constantly monitored cameras to ensure nothing untoward went down—and ensured that the elevator car didn't stop on floors where an enemy might be waiting. An extra layer of protection considering what would happen to anyone who broke Nic's enforced truce, but considering the clientele he catered to, it wasn't nearly as paranoid as it seemed.

Tristan didn't go back to his room. Now that Amarante had arrived, he would be expected to dance to the tune Zhao set. There was no room for error in the next few days, and there sure as fuck wasn't room for casual disobedience. Since Tristan liked having his head attached to his neck, he only stepped out of line when he knew he could get away with it. It happened rarely. Zhao knew he had a nuclear bomb in the form of a person when it came to Tristan, and he only used him when absolutely necessary. The rest of the time, he preferred to keep Tristan close.

It was almost as if he didn't trust him.

He smiled at that. Zhao was too smart to trust Tristan, even after a decade of dancing to whatever tune the old man set. Which just proved he wasn't a fool. The only person Tristan gave complete loyalty to was himself. Working for Zhao served his purpose... until it didn't.

After amusing himself by wandering for a bit, he circled back to one of the restaurants. A drink wasn't out of the question before he made his report. This whole summit reeked of a terrible idea. Zhao couldn't move on Amarante within these walls. Even he wasn't above the Warren's laws, and he was responsible for the actions of the people under his command. He couldn't sacrifice some young idiot to get the job done.

Tristan would like to see one of them try, though. It'd be amusing to watch Amarante take them apart piece by piece. He hadn't seen her fight in years, but she wasn't the type to let such a valuable skillset fall by the wayside. No, she was blade sharp and just as likely to gut a man.

He strode into the restaurant, a carefully cultivated design that conveyed big money while still being bland as fuck so it wouldn't insult anyone. Tristan snorted. The Warren danced on the edge, a constant balancing act to keep everyone slightly—but equally—uncomfortable. Equality was the name of the game, even when it came down to the types of food offered and the color on the walls.

A hostess appeared, a pretty Black girl. She smiled at him. "For one?"

"Just looking for a drink."

"Of course, sir." She pivoted on a low heel and led him deeper into the restaurant. A small table was their destination, tucked against the wall, but not perfectly. Tristan slowed, taking in the room again. The walls… curved.

He laughed. "They really weren't taking any chances here, were they?"

"Sir?"

He waved it away. "Never mind." A curved wall meant no one could quite get their backs to it. There would always be the chance someone could sneak up in their blind spot. Tristan shook his head. This was going to be a long-ass couple of days.

The waitress appeared the second he sat down, a white girl with brilliant red hair. Her smile widened at the sight of him, but Tristan couldn't even enjoy her flirting. Not when his mind was still tangled up in seeing Amarante again. He ordered a beer, and ignored the waitress's disappointment.

Amarante.

As if his thoughts conjured her, she walked through the entranceway and into the restaurant. The hostess tried to intercept her, but Amarante's gaze fell on him and she ignored the other woman to stalk in his direction. And it was a *stalk*. She moved like she fully intended to deliver her namesake. Death. He'd known her before she became one of the so-called Four Horsemen who ruled the Island of Ys, but the role suited her. She was dangerous in the same kind of way Tristan was dangerous.

And, fuck, she was even more beautiful than she'd been at eighteen when he met her. She'd taken the time to change into a pair of tailored black pants and a suit jacket with something funky going on with the shoulders. Beneath it was lace that gave tantalizing glimpses of her golden skin beneath it. Her shoulder-length black hair hung in a perfect curtain that swung a little with each step, and she had some eyeliner shit winging over her eyes, emphasizing their darkness.

She walked to his table and slid into the seat across from him.

Tristan raised his beer in a mocking toast. "By all means, join me."

She took his beer out of his hand and sipped it. The audacity made him grin, but Amarante looked deadly serious. "My brother's fine, in case you were wondering."

"I wasn't." He sat back in his chair, giving all evidence of being relaxed. He wasn't sure he was faster than her. Maybe he had been once, but they hadn't sparred in a long, long time. Tristan couldn't be sure he'd react in time if she struck. He didn't think she'd waste her shot on him, but if he could anticipate her moves that well, they wouldn't be in this situation to begin with.

She took another sip of his beer. "You weren't trying to kill him."

"If I wanted him dead, he would be." Amarante studied him. Her eyes were so fucking cold, he almost believed they could freeze him on the spot. He made a show of looking at himself. "Sorry, the ice gaze isn't a thing outside of comics."

"It's not going to work."

He knew better than to let her bait him, but he wanted to know where she was headed with this. "You don't think so?"

"My father doesn't want peace. You know it as well as I do. He's merely looking for the chance to wipe us off the board once and for all."

Honestly, Tristan agreed with her. There might have been a chance to take the Horsemen off the map ten years ago when they first showed up, but they'd built an empire of their own. Removing them would be messy and it'd draw attention. Neither were things Zhao shunned, but he had his reasons for ignoring them until they forced his hand when *they* started hunting *him.*

"Easier ways to get you dead if that's his goal." The old man's end game was a mystery, but he wasn't in a habit of losing when he wanted something done. He'd ordered Tristan to *take* Ryu. Not to kill him.

She went perfectly still. "Do not tell me that he's attempting some kind of reconciliation. I won't believe it, and you'll just embarrass yourself."

"I'm tired of talking about him, Te." Tristan grinned. "Let's talk about us." He truly enjoyed the way her fingers spasmed the tiniest amount every time he used her old nickname. Amarante may play the part of the ice dragon, but she was flesh and blood just like the rest of them; which meant he could get under her skin.

"There's nothing to talk about."

"Come on, now. I don't think three years and several months of sharing the same bed—"

Amarante moved. She threw his beer at his face before he

could do more than start. Fuck, she was fast. The cold cascaded over him and he blinked at her. "You just ruined my shirt."

"You can afford another one." She turned and held up her hands at the waitress and hostess who'd both appeared the second she moved to attack. Amarante gave a careful smile. "A friendly disagreement. No harm done."

"Except to my shirt."

"You're lucky it wasn't a fork I threw."

A fork wouldn't kill him, but it would hurt like a bitch. He shot her a look and then turned a smile on the waitress and hostess. "No harm done."

The waitress approached slowly. She didn't have a gun on her—none were allowed on the property, even by staff—but she would be trained to take down a threat just like the rest of Nic's people. She looked between them and sighed. "I'll get you another beer. Would you like something, Ms. Death?"

"No, I won't be staying long."

Tristan pulled the wet fabric of his shirt away from his chest. "Dramatic."

"You deserve worse." She was back to being cold again, that flash of heat carefully banked and controlled.

He shouldn't provoke her. He had a job to do, and riling Amarante would make his job harder. Knowing that didn't seem to matter. But then, Tristan had never been that good at denying himself the things he wanted. No, he set his mind on a goal and then he went after it with everything he had until he achieved it. Money, power, women.

There was one exception, one person completely immune to his charms, and she sat across the table from him. He leaned forward. She still felt something. He wouldn't be able to get under her skin so easily otherwise. Whether it was simply hate or something more complicated remained to be seen. He barely dared hope that it was the latter. "I still want you, Te. I never stopped."

"It doesn't matter what you want." She bit out each word. "You made your choice when you went to work for *him*. If I'd known the pain that would cause the people I care about in the future, I would have killed you that day and been done with it."

She meant it. Every word.

Back then, she might have even succeeded. Hell, she might succeed now if they went around. He honestly didn't know which of them was better, and it made him crazy. "You're welcome to make up for the lost opportunity now."

Her lips curved a little, but her eyes went even colder. "Fighting or fucking. That's all you are, Tristan. I enjoyed the entertainment you offered when I was young and foolish, but I know better now. A scorpion cannot help but be a scorpion; no matter how pretty its face, it will sting you the first chance it gets."

Layers beneath layers of her words, but he still couldn't get to the center of it. No matter. He'd just keep poking until he found out what he needed to know. Tristan was rather skilled at provoking people. "So what I'm hearing is that you think I'm pretty."

She planted her hands on the table and rose. "I don't have regrets over the things I've done in my life. They've been necessary in one form or another, and they've served to reach the end game we're playing out right now." Amarante straightened. "I do regret you, though. Only you." She turned and walked away.

Tristan watched her go. The strange ache in his chest had to be from the cold-ass beer making everything miserable. But even as he tried to tell himself that, anger rose, a welcome wave of warmth. She regretted *him*. Fuck that.

Fuck.

That.

He didn't believe in regrets any more than she claimed to. Yeah, he'd stung the untouchable Amarante when things fell out the way they did. He wasn't naive enough to believe otherwise. It didn't change the fact that those few years they were friends—and then more than friends—meant something, and fuck her for acting like they didn't. It wouldn't change their path going forward; nothing could change where they'd ended up now. Knowing that didn't mean Tristan had any intention of letting this lie, though.

He didn't lose control. Too much rested on his ability to get shit done, and messy emotions were exactly that: a mess.

That didn't stop him from pushing to his feet and taking off after Amarante.

He found her heading for the elevators, her walk measured and unhurried. Either she didn't realize he'd follow her, or this was some kind of fucked up power play. He didn't know which he preferred, but the end result was his catching her so Tristan wasn't about to complain. He picked up his pace and reached for her.

He never made contact.

Amarante moved through his fingers like water, spinning on one stupidly tall heel. Fast. She was so fucking *fast*. She grabbed his wrist and pulled a move he should have seen coming a mile away, twisting it between his shoulder blades and shoving his face against the wall.

"Don't touch me." Her voice was just as calm and cold as ever... if someone didn't know her.

Even after all this time, Tristan picked up the tremor beneath. He shifted in her grip and cursed when she wrenched his arm back harder. "You've proven your point."

"I don't think I—"

He didn't give her a chance to finish. Tristan slammed them back against the opposite wall, using his larger size to shove her despite the pain in his arm. Amarante's grip faltered and he spun around.

She punched him in the fucking throat.

Tristan stumbled back with a rasping gasp. "The fuck?"

"I told you not to touch me." She smoothed down her suit jacket, but the ice had cracked and the fire beneath bristled. "You used to be able to take simple instructions."

"Your simple instructions used to be *harder* and *more* and *right there.*"

She looked like she wanted to hit him again. "Stop doing that."

"Doing what?" It hurt to speak, but he didn't give a damn. This might be the last time they could talk alone, and Tristan would say whatever it took to ensure she didn't walk away. Not yet. "Taking a walk down memory lane."

Footsteps sounded, and he knew without a shadow of a doubt that it was Nic's people rushing to ensure he and Amarante didn't kill each other in the hallway. He glared in their direction. "Come on."

"The fuck I will." Fury had worked its way into her words, and he relished that level of reaction.

Tristan held out a hand. "We're about to be dragged before Nic to explain ourselves. I'm not in the mood. Are you?"

She hesitated, but the footsteps were getting closer. "Fine." She ignored his hand and started down the hallway.

Tristan picked up his pace to get in front of her. "This way."

"If you're leading me into a trap, I'll slit your throat myself."

He laughed hoarsely. "That's what I've always loved about you, Te. You're never worried about getting your hands dirty. Come on."

CHAPTER 3

$\mathcal{F}$ollowing Tristan through a door and into a dark room was a mistake. Amarante went out of her way to ensure she didn't make mistakes, but she couldn't seem to help herself where this man was concerned. She stepped into the darkened room and he shut the door behind them. The move put Tristan too close, his body nearly pressing against hers. Moving away meant admitting defeat, and she'd already shown her hand too blatantly.

Tristan took a step back, but she didn't have a chance to appreciate the new distance because he stripped out of his shirt in quick, economical movements. Even in the low light, the sight of him stole her breath. He shouldn't seem larger without his shirt, but he somehow was, each muscle seeming to be cut from stone. He'd never be beautiful, not really, but he was unmistakably powerful.

There isn't enough air in the room.

A silly thought. Of course there was enough air in the room. Her lungs worked, even as her mind spun back upon itself, inhaling and exhaling just like they'd been doing since her birth. This wasn't a physical reaction, not in the way her brain wanted her to think it was. No, this was just pheromones and her responding on a cellular level to Tristan's presence. It was *science*.

Knowing that didn't make the winch tightening around her chest any looser. Why was she here? Not here in the Warren, but here in this room. She had no reason to run with Tristan, no logical reason to follow his rough order. "This was a mistake."

"Te." She hadn't seen him move, but he was suddenly closer, boxing her in with his presence even though she could *clearly* see a path to the door. Tristan lowered his voice, and it was just like so many nights all those years ago, when their careful friendship had shifted into something else entirely. Right before it ended. "You look good, Te. Really good."

"Don't do that."

"Don't do what?"

This close, she caught the scent of beer on his skin from the one she'd doused him with. Beneath it, the faint spicy cologne he'd worn since they were barely more than children. She cleared her throat, hating that she gave him even that much response. "You know what."

Tristan looked down at her for a long moment, the tension spinning out between them as their exhales mingled. She held her breath out of spite, and his answering grin told her that he knew exactly why she'd done it.

"So. Not just hate." Tristan shifted closer yet before she could ask him what the hell he was talking about. He still managed to hold himself back from actually touching her. "I'm going to kiss you now."

"No, you aren't."

He planted his hands on the wall on either side of her head and leaned down to speak in her ear. "Every time the ice cracks, I see you, Te. That wall is fucking impressive, but we both know what lies beneath. You want this as much as I do."

She was very, very afraid he was right.

That's why Amarante, the woman who had never met a situation she couldn't scheme her way out of, panicked. She sucker punched him, sinking every bit of momentum she could into the hit. Tristan's breath left him in a rush, but he didn't go down. Of course he didn't go down. The man was a modern gladiator, a machine whose sole purpose was death. *Her* namesake. She couldn't think about that right now, just like she couldn't think about exactly how much she wanted him to follow through on his stated intentions.

No, she had to get out of this room and she had to get out now. Tomorrow she would see her father for the first time since she was seven years old, and she needed her head on straight. She could *not* make mistakes. Except she couldn't keep from doing exactly that. She bolted for the door like a lamb fleeing the slaughter.

Of course Tristan caught her. If she was thinking clearly, she never would have presented him with her back. He snagged her around the waist, but she was already turning, striking out blindly, two decades of training taking over her body even as her mind turned into a staticky buzz. She elbowed him in the stomach and stomped her stiletto heel into the top of his foot. Tristan cursed, but didn't release her. "Stop being an idiot."

Amarante didn't lose her temper.

She couldn't afford to. She was too deadly and there were too many people depending on her to keep them safe. Her siblings, yes, but every employee at the Island of Ys came there with the assurance that she would ensure they remained safe for the duration of their time on the island. She fought and planned and killed to create the only place in this world that was safe for her and the others. Letting something as mundane as anger derail that was unacceptable.

Tristan's words snapped a leash she thought cast in stone. Literal red washed over her vision and she reached back and grabbed his balls. His curse cut off when she squeezed. The fabric of the slacks kept her from digging her nails in, but she would without hesitation. Any advantage was fair game, no matter how cruel and underhanded. "Let. Me. Go."

He dropped his hands immediately. But the second she went to move away, he tackled her to the floor. "That was a shitty move." The bastard barely sounded out of breath.

She twisted and fought and clawed, but he used his superior weight to keep her pinned beneath him, to maneuver her body until his whole weight pressed between her thighs. She couldn't move more than a few inches in any direction, and the friction from it had her senses shorting out in confusion. Amarante went slack, panting like an animal in a trap. "I should have ripped them off."

"Aw, Te, you say the sweetest things." *He'd* recovered fast. He snagged her wrists when she went for his eyes and pinned them on either side of her head. Tristan grinned, his white teeth flashing in the dimness of the room. "If you ripped off my balls, you wouldn't be able to play with them later."

Her jaw dropped. "You're out of your fucking mind. The only way I'd touch you is with a knife in my hand."

If anything, his grin widened. "Like I said; the sweetest things."

She tried to slide out from beneath him, but he had her too effectively pinned. Amarante glared up at Tristan, trying and failing not to notice how hard his cock had become. The confused zinging in her body only intensified. "We're enemies."

"Yep." It didn't sound like it bothered him in the least, but then the truth of the world had never gotten in the way of Tristan going after what he wanted. Why should that change now? He didn't move, didn't do anything but hold her down and suffocate her with his overwhelming presence. She could taste him on the back of her tongue, and even though Amarante knew it was only a trick of the mind, she couldn't help licking her lips.

When was the last time she'd had someone affect her on this level?

Even Cora, her friend and lover over the years, came with a certain set of expectations. Their respective responsibilities meant that they could never let each other too close, and she'd made her peace with that a long time ago. Her life required sacrifices and she'd never made qualms about that. Let others have their regrets and their desire for happiness. Safety and revenge were the only two gods she worshiped, and when forced to choose between them, she would always choose the latter. It was the entire reason she was in the Warren in the first place.

Her body wasn't listening, though. The sheer weight of Tristan, of his presence, uncoiled something dark and dangerous in her. Something she couldn't afford to let loose. "Tristan, please." She didn't know what she was asking for. To be let up. For more. Something else entirely.

He gave her no quarter. "Please what?"

She hated him in that moment. Not a new feeling, not when he was one of the few people she'd let close enough to hurt her who actually hurt her. But this was new and hot and twisted up in desire and betrayal and need. "Kiss me or get the hell off me."

For a breadth of a heartbeat, he didn't move and she thought for sure he would twist this around on her as well. Laugh that he'd managed to ruffle Death herself. Maybe finish the attack with a dose of humiliation. Something.

Then his mouth crashed down on hers and Amarante stopped thinking entirely. He tried to take her mouth, but she was too busy taking his right back. She was not the conquered in this scenario, and the sooner he realized it, the better.

Tristan laughed against her lips. "Difficult."

"Arrogant."

He kissed her again and thrust his hips against hers, dragging his cock along her center in a slow glide. It was so good. Too good. He released her wrists and ran his hands down her body, wedging them beneath her ass to lift her hips and give him a better angle. The next thrust ground directly against her clit. If she let him keep going, she might actually come from something as mundane as dry humping on the floor. And she didn't care.

What the hell was *wrong* with her? She pulled away from his kiss. "Tristan, wait."

"I missed you, Te." He pushed her jacket off her shoulders and cupped one breast. Was it her imagination or did his breath catch a little as he teased her nipple to a point through her shirt? It must be. Surely it was all in her head. If Tristan was that affected by simply touching her, he never would have done what he did. She had to get up, had to stop this right now before she gave away every advantage she desperately needed. Tristan was the enemy now, even if once upon a time, he'd been a friend. She couldn't trust him, could all but be assured that anything that happened between her and him would be reported directly back to the man he answered to.

The man she came here to kill.

The thought was a bucket of cold water dousing her desire. She shoved at his shoulders. "Get off me, Tristan. Right fucking now."

He hesitated and for a moment she despaired—hoped—

he'd ignore her. But he moved back quickly, obviously expecting her to kick him in the balls. "You want this."

No point in lying when she'd been grinding on him like the horny teenagers they once were. "My body wants this." Amarante rose to her feet and smoothed down her clothing. "My brain knows better."

He gave her a cocky grin that she wanted to slap right off his face. "Give your brain a rest, Te. It's got to be tired after all that scheming."

"You wouldn't know. Your master says jump and you ask how high."

The amusement drained from his face, leaving the same version of Tristan who'd told her that if she made him choose between her and Zhao, he'd go with Zhao. The memory still hurt, even though she'd revisited it enough that time should have dulled its edges. She embraced the pain. This was what she needed, the reminder of how little she could trust him. She didn't usually need to learn the same lesson twice, but there was a first time for everything.

He walked to the spot where he'd dropped his shirt and scooped it up, though he made no move to cover his chest. "This summit isn't going to go the way you want it to."

"Of that, I have no doubt." The way she *wanted* it to go was for her to successfully cut the head off the operation that stole children and stuffed them into places where their abusers paid top dollar for the privilege. Until they dealt with her father, the man responsible, they could spend the rest of their lives killing his subordinates without making a single damn difference. The only option was to go straight to the top.

His expression didn't flicker. For someone who called her an ice queen, he certainly had his emotions locked down when he wasn't playing the part of the charming rogue. "He only wants to talk, Te."

Sheer rage stole her breath. It took several long moments for her to wrestle herself back under control. "You don't get to tell me what he wants. If this is all part of his plan to set me off balance—"

"It's not."

She gave him the incredulous look that statement deserved. "This was a mistake. We're finished."

"I thought we were." His expression went contemplative. "But I guess I was wrong. That changes things."

His stubbornness made her want to throw things. Tristan had never troubled himself with things like right or wrong; there was only what he wanted and what he didn't. Amarante didn't hold that against him, not when she had a similar line to determine her values. No, what she held against him was his willingness to try to force her hand.

"It changes nothing." She moved to the door, but couldn't stop herself from saying, "He put my brother and me in that place, Tristan. We would have died there and he wouldn't have blinked. He's done worse to others over the years, and *you work for him*." She walked out the door before he could say something else to dig his way under her skin.

Too late for that. Much too late. Tristan Merrick had been under her skin from the day they met. The only thing that mattered now was ensuring that truth didn't divert her from her plans.

Kill her father.

Save her family.

That was the only thing that mattered.

CHAPTER 4

*T*ristan waited several long minutes after Amarante walked out of the room to do the same. He didn't usually waste time with regrets, but he'd fucked up this interaction. There was no other way to look at it. Oh, Zhao would pat him on the back for disrupting the enemy before negotiations, but that hadn't been a strategy he intentionally deployed. Not with Amarante.

He wasn't even remotely surprised to find Nic waiting for him in the hallway. "Don't you have bigger shit to worry about than babysitting me?"

Nic pushed off the wall and fell into step next to him. "I have half a dozen things demanding my attention right now, yes, but you're the only idiot who seems intent on breaking my rules."

Couldn't argue that, but the best policy was to refuse to admit anything. "Not sure what you're talking about."

Nic snorted. "Do you really think there's a single room in this place that isn't wired with half a dozen cameras and microphones?"

"Nothing happened." Nothing he'd wanted to, anyways.

He and Amarante had been on a collision course since the moment things went to shit ten years ago. It was just a matter of where and when. They were too well matched to move through the world without finding each other again. In all that time, he'd thought they were destined for confrontation. He'd never dared hope that she'd still want him.

And she did want him. She might hate it, but that kiss told him everything he needed to know.

"Tristan." The tone of his friend's voice slowed him down. Nic slid his hands into his pockets, green eyes serious. "If you can't keep your shit together, you're out until this is over. I don't give a fuck that you're Zhao's man or a friend. If you step out of line, I'll have to make an example of you." He wouldn't enjoy it, but he'd do it all the same. Nic took his responsibilities as head of the Warren deadly seriously.

Tristan respected that. He did. He'd just never been one for following the rules. "It was just a bit of foreplay."

Nic's brows rose. "She was two seconds from ripping your balls off. Literally."

"Like I said—foreplay."

"You'll forgive me if I don't take your word for it."

Tristan waved that away. "Talk to her. If she isn't on the same page, you can string me up for everyone to see." She *was* on the same page. Amarante was his equal in every way. They just never fought before. Not like this. When they were younger, it was so fucking easy to just *be* with her. Tristan didn't have friends. Oh, he had Nic. They were two sides to the same coin, and they understood each other perfectly. That kind of thing didn't happen often, especially not in the world they moved in. But aside from that, he preferred to keep the human filth he interacted with at a distance.

When he knew Amarante before, there was none of that bullshit. They shared a perfect understanding that he hadn't realized was rare until he lost it. He couldn't repair her trust.

He wouldn't waste his time in trying. But Amarante was too practical to let something as mundane as trust get in the way of what she wanted.

She wanted him. She didn't *want* to want him, but the attraction between them was even stronger than it had been before.

"Tristan."

He realized Nic had stopped walking and he'd kept moving. A lapse Tristan knew better than to make. Friend or no, Nic would stab him in the back if it meant preserving the sanctity of his precious Warren. "Talk to her if you need to. She'll confirm it."

"Tristan."

He cursed and turned around to find Nic watching him closely. "What?"

"She's the one?"

Tristan wasn't the type to delve into syrupy emotions and pour his heart out, but one night he and Nic had drank themselves stupid and one confession led to another. It was the reason he knew Nic's parents were a mechanic and a kindergarten teacher who lived in a little town in Ohio. Tristan had never told his friend her name, but he'd talked about the girl who turned into something more than friends before it all burned down around them. A lie danced on the tip of his tongue, a change of subject to prevent anyone from getting too close to this truth. But this was *Nic*. They might end up as enemies before the end of this, but at least they were fucking honest with each other. "She's the one."

"Fuck."

"Yeah, pretty much."

Nic ran a hand through his short dark hair. "This is going to blow up in everyone's faces. You want to chase her down, you do it after the summit."

Tristan wasn't so sure there would actually be an *after* the summit. He didn't know Zhao's plans. The man was hardly transparent under normal circumstances, but for the last few months, he'd been a vault. He gave orders, and he didn't tolerate anyone questioning him. It all centered around his growing obsession with the Horsemen of the Island of Ys, two of which were his children.

That Tristan hadn't expected. He still didn't know how to wrap his head around the fact that Zhao allowed two of his children to exist in that fucking camp of his. He didn't understand, but he wasn't paid to understand, he was paid to follow orders. No one asked him what he thought of this clusterfuck, but why would they?

"Cards to your chest, Nic."

He narrowed his eyes. "You're unsanctioned? Jesus fuck, Tristan, are you out of your mind? Bad enough when I thought it was a ploy to undermine her before tomorrow. The old man doesn't know what you're up to?"

He'd already said too much. "Cards to your chest," he repeated.

"No shit, cards to my chest." Nic took a breath and his expression smoothed out. "Go back to your room. I don't want to see you again until the first meeting tomorrow, and I sure as hell better not see you without your escort again."

As if that would stop him.

He knew better than to say as much aloud, though. Friends or not, Nic wouldn't let a little thing like their history get in the way of doing his job. If he thought for a second that Tristan would endanger the summit, he'd kick his ass to the curb. Tristan *might* be able to get past all the security in the Warren with a year of planning and a team of four with a particular blend of skills, but by then it would be too late and whatever was going to happen with Zhao and Amarante would have already gone down.

No, he needed to be here. He couldn't let his personal bullshit distract him.

He gave Nic a charming smile. "I'll be a good boy."

"You're a goddamn liar." They stopped in front of the elevator and Nic stabbed the button. "Directly to your room. I don't have any patience left tonight."

He couldn't give his word that he'd behave for the duration of the summit. He already knew he wouldn't. But he could give Nic tonight. "I promise."

"You are a pain in my ass, you know that?"

"Indubitably."

"Asshole," Nic muttered. He waited for Tristan to step into the elevator and press his hand to the scanner. "Enjoy your beauty rest."

"Yeah, yeah." He didn't slump back against the wall after the elevator doors closed, but he wanted to. Now that his adrenaline was bottoming out, his balls fucking ached from where Amarante had grabbed them. A shady ass move and he admired her all the more for doing it. Winning at any cost was the name of the game. Normal people didn't like hearing that shit. They wanted things to be fair and easy and not rock the boat too much. More normal people hadn't reached the sheer levels of desperation Tristan had as a kid. The same levels Amarante had experienced, though she'd never admit as much now.

Winning at any cost.

He'd do well to remember that.

He wasn't even surprised to find Kale standing there when the doors opened. The big Samoan man towered over everyone in any room he walked into, but he looked particularly large in the narrow hallway. He didn't return Tristan's easy smile, but then he never did. "Boss man wants you."

Tristan let his grin fall away. He didn't need to play pretend for these people. The only things they responded to were fear and power, and he had both in spades. A decade of doing whatever was required of him had created a reputation that only the most foolish in Zhao's organization were willing to fuck with. It didn't stop people from trying at times, but the challenges to his authority had decreased as the years went on. Tristan wasn't stupid enough to let down his guard, though. "By all means, lead the way."

Kale turned and strode to the end of the hall. He was light on his feet for such a big man, a fact that always surprised his enemies. His size led them to underestimate them, and he took full advantage of it. Tristan made a habit never to tangle with Kale if he could avoid it. The man hit like a freight train.

They'd set up Zhao in the suite that seemed large enough to encompass half the floor. The Warren was tricky, though. Because only part of it was exposed to the mountainside and the rest was inside the mountain itself, no one knew exactly how big it was or had anything resembling blueprints. It had been designed that way, but it still irritated Tristan not to know all the exits. Add in the secondary set of ways to get around that only Nic and his staff used, and it was impossible to map.

He slipped off his shoes after he walked through the door and headed to where Zhao sat in front of a fireplace taller than he was. The Chinese man was built shorter and more delicately than either of his children, but he exuded power and danger more than anyone Tristan had ever met. He turned as Tristan approached and took in his shirtless state. "Trouble?"

"Nothing I couldn't handle, sir." The bowing and scraping and politicking weren't Tristan's favorite, but he'd learned to fake it in order to climb the ranks. Now the faux deference came as second nature when he was in this man's presence. "She arrived a few hours ago, and she came alone like you suspected she would." Zhao's little game of bait and switch with his children had paid off. The other three Horsemen had gone to NYC to deal with the threat Tristan presented, clearing the way for Amarante—for Death—to come here without interference.

It spoke volumes that Zhao went through such lengths to separate them.

"Good." Zhao folded his hands, appearing perfectly relaxed. A lie that Tristan wasn't foolish enough to believe. He'd seen the man order countless deaths with that same calm expression on his face. "You know your task, Tristan. I trust you won't disappoint me."

"Of course not, sir." He kept any annoyance from his face. "I'll keep Death distracted." He was grateful for the command, if only because it gave him the freedom to do what he was already planning on doing—pursue Amarante.

Zhao turned to look at the large screen that took up the wall opposite the door. It served the purpose of a window, showing a snowy mountainside even though they were encased completely in rock. A lie, but a good one from the technology. If he didn't get close enough to examine it, he might have believed they had one of the outward facing rooms…that didn't exist. All guest rooms in the Warren were enclosed.

The better to keep the occupants safe—and from endangering others with nighttime escapades.

"Tristan, I like you."

The small hairs on the back of his neck stood at attention. This was bad. "I'm glad to hear that, sir."

"I would be devastated to lose you. You're an invaluable member of my organization." Zhao slowly rotated back to face him. He still looked calm and relaxed, but there was no denying the threat. "If you touch my daughter, I'll be forced to take action."

Considering Amarante's taste still lingered on his tongue

—considering he fully intended to kiss her again at the earliest opportunity—he managed to keep his reaction under wraps. "I understand, sir."

"There are times when I will allow you to bend within the boundaries of my command. This is not one of them. She's not meant for you."

Only years of training kept Tristan from asking who the fuck Zhao thought Amarante was *meant for*. He knew what this summit was about. The old man had his plans within plans within plans, and he always had. He wanted something from the daughter he'd sent to hell as a child, and he'd do whatever it took to ensure he reached the objective he sought.

Was he trying to bring her back into the fold? Surely not. Tristan would never have considered Zhao delusional, but he was exactly that if he thought Amarante would bend a knee to him. She was far more likely to cut him off at them.

He realized he hadn't responded and cleared his throat. "I understand, sir."

Zhao studied him for a long moment. His dark eyes were so similar to Amarante's, though he doubted either of them would appreciate the comparison. Finally, Zhao nodded, almost to himself. "You'll sit at my right hand tomorrow. Ensure that you're not late."

"Yes, sir."

This time, when Zhao turned around, it was an obvious dismissal. Tristan didn't allow himself to sigh in relief. He simply nodded at Kale, collected his shoes, and walked out the door. He kept his strides even as he moved down the hall to his room. It was only when he closed the door that he allowed the tiniest bit of steam to release. "That motherfucker."

She's not meant for you.

Twelve years working for Zhao, and it hardly all boiled

down to this, but it fucking stung. He threw his daughter away like trash, like worse than trash, because at least trash isn't tortured and abused for years on end. She could have died in that camp. Tristan had looked into it quietly a few months ago when he realized that *Zhao* was the one responsible for Camp Bueller. Finding information was difficult. When the camp was shut down, it was *shut down* as if it'd never existed aside from a rumor. The adults there were cockroaches fleeing the light. The children?

Even as cold as he was, there were lines that shouldn't be crossed. Camp Bueller crossed every single one of them gleefully.

He stopped. Inhaled. Exhaled.

At the end of the day, it didn't fucking matter what Zhao wanted. It didn't even matter what Amarante wanted. Everyone was in the Warren with their own agenda, and that included Tristan.

What he wanted above all else was *Amarante*.

CHAPTER 5

Even though Amarante knew it was coming, she wasn't prepared for the twisting in her stomach when the phone in her room rang. Maybe if she'd slept better last night, she'd feel calmer. Or if she hadn't grappled with Tristan until their mouths found each other and only remembered herself at last moment. She needed her thoughts in order for the meeting in an hour, but first she had to head this argument off at the pass.

Her voice was perfectly even when she answered. "Yes?"

"I don't fucking believe you."

She closed her eyes and strove for calm. Ryu, her little brother. "Did you have any problems getting back to the island?"

Someone made a noise perilously close to a growl and she realized she was on speaker phone with *all* her siblings. Sure enough, Luca spoke next. "We're getting on the next plane up there. Don't do anything until we arrive."

"No." The word came out too sharp, but there was no going back now. "I've already instructed Nicholai not to grant you entrance or it will cause an incident."

"Then I'm about to cause a fucking incident, Te. You promised to give us time to figure out a way to him without endangering you."

She swallowed hard. Thankfully, they couldn't see her, or they'd know she wasn't nearly as collected as she wanted to be. Her cracks were showing in a way she couldn't afford. "I lied."

Now it was Kenzie's turn to pile on. "Screw Nicholai. I'll kick his ass and then I'm going to kick yours. You *lied*. Fuck, Amarante, you know better than that. We lie to everyone else. Not to each other."

They didn't understand. They never really would, no matter how they tried. Ryu may be her brother by blood, but Luca and Kenzie where her siblings in every other way, too. They had suffered more while they were in Camp Bueller than anyone should suffer over the course of a lifetime. And now, against all logic, they were *happy*. They had partners. Luca and Cami would be starting a family shortly. They deserved peace and more.

She was the only one who could ensure that it would happen.

"He has an army, Kenzie." Ryu sounded more tired than she'd ever heard him. "Every single person in that place is trained to kill, and they all answer to him. There's no getting through. That's the point."

"But—"

He charged right over her, as relentless as the tide. "Even if you did manage to get to Zhao, even if you killed him, Amarante has presented herself as our leader. She still dies."

"That is so *fucked*."

Luca made that growling noise again. "Come home, Te. We'll find another way. You're not alone, no matter how much you like to pretend you're the only one who can get the job done. There are other options."

She truly wished there were. "If that were the case, we'd have found them by now." Amarante closed her eyes and forced every bit of weakness from her voice. She couldn't afford for them to doubt her, not when their very lives rode on them obeying. "Stay on the island. This will be over soon." She hesitated. "I love you." She hung up before they could get out their sea of protests.

If she concentrated, she could almost convince herself that her hand didn't shake as she replaced the phone in its cradle. On second thought... she lifted the receiver and pushed the button to take her to the Warren's staff. A man answered, his voice deep and calm. "Good morning, Ms. Death. How may I be of service?"

The reminder of who she was centered her. Death did not falter. "My siblings may attempt to contact me. Please take messages but do not forward their calls to my room." This would be difficult enough without them attempting to dissuade her. There was no altering this course she'd set herself on. One way or another, hers would be the hand that took Zhao Fai down. Now the only thing that remained was ensuring none of her siblings were harmed in the process. They had too much to live for now. She wouldn't allow them to torpedo their lives for her.

"Of course. We'll see it done." The man paused. "Would you like me to pass on any message to Nicholai?"

"Yes. Please tell him to remember our terms and not to allow any of the other Horsemen on the grounds for the duration of the summit."

"I will."

"Thank you." She hung up, but taking that step did nothing to quell the nervous energy sparking at her nerve endings. So many years' work would come to fruition in thirty minutes. It seemed surreal, and for the first time in longer than she cared to remember, she wasn't sure how things would play out. Zhao—her father—had been an enigma in so many ways. A powerful man. Now she knew him to be an evil man, too, but that didn't surprise her. No one came to that much power with clean hands. But the sheer scope of his sins left her breathless if she thought about it too hard.

She rose and walked to the full-length mirror. She'd dressed carefully for this meeting. Her three piece suit was deceptively feminine, from the wide-legged pants that would allow her free movement if she needed to fight to the reinforced panels in the vest that would protect her torso from the worst of any blows. It wouldn't stop a bullet, but it didn't need to in the Warren. No guns allowed. Her heels were high enough to be weapons all of their own, but that was the only thing she had on her person. They had searched her luggage like she knew they would—the Island of Ys did the same thing—and so she hadn't tried to sneak any conventional weapons in.

She touched the pen tucked into the pocket on the inside of her jacket. A pen, yes. It even wrote. But it contained a poison that, when injected, would result in death within two minutes.

She was as ready as she'd ever be. Anything more was simply procrastinating and showing up late was out of the question.

Amarante took a slow breath all the way down to the bottom of her lungs, held it for a few seconds, and released it slowly. There could be no mistakes. She had to do this perfectly, which was a special kind of hell since she still wasn't quite sure why Zhao had set up this meeting. It was entirely possible it was all a scheme to get her out of the safety of the island to where he could take her out, but he'd instructed Tristan to actually *take* Ryu.

She didn't understand, and she didn't like that she didn't understand.

And Tristan?

There was no use thinking about Tristan at all. Last night was a fluke. It had to be. Fight or flight did strange things to a body's chemistry, releasing chemicals that could confuse a person. It's the only reason fighting almost turned to fucking. Knowing that would help her keep her guard up. Tristan had betrayed her. There was no going back after that; not to friendship and certainly not to the kind of trust required for sex. A person was vulnerable when they were intimate with another in the most basic way possible. She couldn't allow it to happen with him.

Again.

She opened her door and stopped at the sight of a young Chinese woman standing there wearing a simple and elegant black suit. She was almost the same height as Amarante and her hair was done in a similarly simple style, though the length was a little shorter. She held out a hand. "Nari. I'll be your escort while you're on the premises."

Amarante shook her hand. "My escort and body double?"

Nari smiled. "Nicholai likes to plan for every eventuality. It's a simple precaution and almost certainly unnecessary."

Almost certainly unnecessary *wasn't* the same thing as being sure, but she could appreciate Nicholai's thoroughness. After all, she'd have done the same thing if she ran an organization like this. "Do all guests receive this extra layer of protection?"

"No."

That answered that. He wasn't certain everyone would play by the rules. Amarante nodded. There was no use asking further questions and delaying her arrival. She wouldn't know entirely what she was dealing with until she walked into that room, no matter how she'd attempted to prepare herself. "We should get moving then."

Nari fell into step beside her, and within ten feet was mirroring her way of walking perfectly. It was strange and uncanny and Amarante didn't like it in the least. She kept her silence.

Five minutes later, they stopped in front of the same plain black door Nicholai had shown her last night. No sound came from within, but that spoke more to the sound proofing than to it being empty.

Nari touched the door handle. "Two Warren representatives will be present during all negotiations as is our policy. If you make any attempt to break the rules, I will stop you using whatever force required, up to and including death."

"I understand." All she had to do was keep breathing, keep her calmness wrapped around her like a shield. It had never been a problem before, but she'd never been in this situation before. She had no other option but pushing forward.

"Good." Nari opened the door and walked into the room, holding it wide so Amarante could follow her.

There were only three people in the large room. The lean Black man stood behind two men sitting at the table, and she took him in quickly because he was easiest. Another Warren employee, present to prevent things from becoming messy. Her gaze fell on Tristan next. He wore another expensive suit with the same carelessness of the one yesterday. To him, clothing only served the most basic purpose. He didn't need it like armor the way Amarante did. Tristan thought he was fucking bulletproof. He didn't smile at her, didn't give any indication that he'd been grinding on her less than twelve hours ago. Good. She had enough to deal with without having to dance around her misstep with him.

There was nowhere else to focus but on the older Chinese man to Tristan's left. She'd seen pictures of Zhao Fai, but somehow they didn't do him justice. Even sitting quietly while she stood, he exuded the kind of power that left her breathless. Amarante spent all her time around dangerous men. Her brothers were two of them. She never doubted that she was the more ruthless, the more *dangerous*, the one who others feared above all else.

That was no longer true.

He didn't rise as she strode to the table, just took her in the same way she took him in. Amarante hated that she could see evidence of herself on his face, of Ryu. It was there in the slope of his nose, the shape of his face, the way his lips quirked the tiniest bit under her regard. Her father and the devil who dominated her past, all wrapped up in a single package she wanted nothing more than to crush into oblivion.

Instead she smiled and sank down to perch on her chair. She hadn't called this meeting, so she would not be the first one speaking. It may seem petty, but bending even such a small amount this early would spell disaster. She still didn't know what he wanted, and until she did, she couldn't plan appropriately.

Amarante eyed the Warren employee behind Zhao. Between that man and Tristan, there was no way she could get to him before they stopped her. The pen worked similar to an EpiPen. It needed a full five seconds in place after it was injected for a lethal dose. Between Tristan and the other, she might get one, if she could even make contact. No, attacking now was out of the question. She had to play the game until she found a better opportunity.

The silence ticked out in seconds and minutes, until Zhao finally smiled. That smile *hurt*. It was like looking at an older version of her brother after a life well-lived. She hated it. She hated that he'd flourished at the suffering of innocents. Her siblings thought his putting his own children into that place was the worst of his sins. Amarante felt differently. They hadn't deserved it. Of course they hadn't deserved it. But better she and Ryu shoulder that burden than the hundreds of other kids who came into that place, never to leave.

Dark thoughts, but then that was her existence. Dark and darker.

Zhao leaned back, seeming perfectly at ease. "You surprise me." He considered her as if she'd only just now walked into the room, rather than been sitting here for damn near ten minutes. "But then, you've always been a bit of a spider in her web, haven't you? You get that from me."

I get nothing *from you.* She barely kept the words locked down. He wanted an emotional response and she refused to give it to him. Amarante studied her nails. "If you wanted small talk, you could have picked up a phone."

He chuckled, the very image of an indulgent father. "I think we both know that wouldn't have gone the way I wanted."

"We'll never know."

"I suppose we won't." He kept smiling, but the humor bled out of his eyes. "It's time to come home, Amarante. For both you and your brother."

Shock shorted out her thoughts. Amarante prided herself on being several steps ahead of everyone else in the room. It was the only way to operate when so much hung in the balance. She'd prepared herself for threats, for assassination, for violence. She'd even considered that he'd try to pay her off to avoid dealing with the Horsemen's vendetta. Not this. Never this. "What did you say?"

"Come home." He spread his arms a little as if in welcome. "You've more than proven yourself worthy of holding the position of heir."

She couldn't breathe. Against every bit of training she had, she glanced at Tristan, but he looked just as confused as she was before he locked down his expression. There would be no clarification from that corner, but she shouldn't have expected it. Amarante refocused on Zhao. When she spoke, only the tiniest bit of hoarseness in her voice betrayed her. "You expect me to believe that the last twenty-five years were all some kind of intricate proving ground."

"I don't particularly care what you believe, daughter. It's time to come home."

He kept saying that, his tone imperial, as if he honestly expected her to bow and scrape at his feet for the honor. Amarante sat back, the only bit of movement she'd allow herself despite the frantic energy bubbling up beneath her skin. She would not let it surface. She would *not*. "I'm not interested in your offer."

"It's not an offer. It's a command to step into the role waiting for you." His smile never faltered, all fake warmth and amusement at her antics. His eyes stayed so, so cold.

Just like hers were when she looked in the mirror after dealing with anyone who wasn't her family.

Stop it. Stop comparing yourself to this man. He may share your blood, but he is not your father and you would never facilitate the kind of evil he has.

All Amarante's victims were willing, people with more money than sense who came to her island. They knew the risks when they walked into her territory, and if they lost something in the mix, they had only themselves to blame. They were adults with free will. They were *not* children snatched from their homes or sold by their families.

Zhao leaned forward and propped his elbows on the table. "You're still harboring anger. It's to be expected, but it's not serving a purpose at this point. Let it go."

Let it go.

As if it was really that easy. Just shuck off ten years of pain and fear and literal torture. Another fifteen of clawing her way to the top and bringing her siblings with her, of doing whatever it took to ensure they were never at another person's mercy ever again.

Rage crystalized inside her, banishing the confusion and shock. She'd feel it later when she was alone, would take it out and pick it apart until she felt in control again. She didn't have that luxury right now. "Did you have an offer? Or were you just planning on issuing a command and hoping for the best?"

He chuckled. "Yes, daughter, I have an offer. You and your brother come back to my estate in China. You're welcomed home like the prodigal children, and you assume the place meant for you as my right hand."

"Your right hand." She flicked a glance at Tristan. He'd shut down completely, his expression offering her nothing but a blank slate. No way to tell what he was thinking about all this. "I was under the impression that the position's filled."

"Ah, that." Zhao waved it away. "Tristan is meant to serve. You are meant to rule. Our operations are a family affair. No outsider will inherit."

There were times, when she was young and scared and trying so desperately hard to be strong for the others, when she would have crawled over broken glass for an offer like this. To be the honored daughter with a destiny. To put aside all the responsibilities she carried on her shoulders, at least for a little while.

She wasn't that scared girl anymore.

"And if I decline?"

"You won't."

The sheer audacity of him made her laugh. "Does every person you meet fall over themselves to do whatever you want?"

"Call it a side effect of the position." He straightened. "But I'm feeling magnanimous. Allow me to convince you."

A brilliant play, really. He knew she wouldn't agree outright. He wasn't a stupid man, and he would have prepared for any eventuality just like she did. Whether this whole production was meant to seduce her back into the fold or simply let her guard down so he could remove her... In the end, it didn't matter.

She'd come to finish this, and that meant she had to dance to his tune.

At least temporarily.

Amarante smiled. "By all means, convince me."

CHAPTER 6

*T*ristan didn't believe in hell, but if it existed, it was a dinner with Amarante and Zhao. They filled the space with carefully curated sentences and barbed words, both trying to edge around each other without offering anything in return. It was fucking exhausting. Give him a straight fight over this politicking and he was a happy man. He could play the game, but he resented the need to.

Playing the game with *Amarante* was a special kind of torment.

Dinner came to a close without either of them giving up anything, but it was only the first day. There were four more where this came from, a small eternity and nowhere near long enough. He had no intention of following Zhao's orders to keep his hands off her. Whether she intended to or not, Amarante had opened the door on them. The tiniest of opportunities, but Tristan had worked with worse odds over the years. Amarante was worth the risk. More than worth it.

While he was considering how the hell he'd get her alone again, Amarante and her escort left the room first. Zhao took a sip of his wine, considering the door she'd just walked through. "She'll come around."

Tristan doubted it. Zhao was used to people doing whatever he wanted and trying to anticipate his needs. Amarante bowed to no one. She had her own reasons for being here and they had nothing to do with angling for a position within the Zhao empire. Saying as much wouldn't earn him any favors, though. "Yes, sir."

Zhao chuckled. "Go entertain yourself. I know how you hate to sit still."

Tristan didn't have a father. Oh, he had one somewhere, but the man hadn't stuck around longer than it took to be a sperm donor. His mother hadn't stayed long enough for him to have memories of her, either. Such was the way of his world, and he didn't waste time and energy bemoaning it. He knew better than to look at Zhao as a stand-in for a parental figure, but the old man liked to play the part when it suited him. "Guilty."

He made it three steps before Zhao's voice stopped him. "I'll be incredibly disappointed if you do something to negatively affect my plans for this summit."

Tristan fought down a flare of anger at the man's words. By the time he turned around, he had his mask in place. "Of course, sir. I wouldn't dream of it. I'm going to find Nic and get into a little sanctioned trouble."

Zhao gave him a long look. "Don't be late tomorrow."

"Yes, sir." He made a swift exit and headed away from the elevators. With each step, his irritation threatened to get the better of him. First he sent Tristan to play distraction, and now he wanted him to stay away from her. What the fuck did Zhao think he was going to accomplish with this? Tristan had thought it was a simple intimidation meeting to get the Horsemen to back off. The other three could burn for all he cared, but his wouldn't be the hand that lifted against Amarante.

But this? This was something else altogether. Surely Zhao realized that Amarante wouldn't play ball, and she sure as fuck wouldn't be softened up into forgiving him the legion of sins committed against her.

He wound his way deeper into the Warren, needing movement more than he needed a destination. He turned a corner and stopped short. His surprised lasted only as long as it took for him to realize it was Nari standing in the hallway, not Amarante. They only looked similar on a superficial level—both Chinese with a slim build and long straight black hair—but that hesitation would have meant his death if that's what Nic wanted.

What the hell was she doing here? Amarante should be back in her room by now.

He noted the studied way Nari slouched against the wall near a nondescript door. Ah. So Amarante hadn't gone back to her room after all. He walked forward slowly, giving Nari plenty of time to see him coming. As if she hadn't clocked him the second he rounded the corner. It was professional courtesy, that's all. "Nari."

"Keep walking, Tristan." If he needed further confirmation that Amarante was behind that door, her words gave it to him.

He held up his hands, painting an innocent expression on his face. "I'm just looking to talk."

"That's bullshit. You know the rules." She didn't have an obvious weapon on her, but she didn't need one. Nari was one of Nic's best. Tristan was relatively sure he could take her down if he needed to, but relatively sure wasn't one hundred percent.

"Death has no need to fear me."

Nari rolled her eyes. "No shit, really?" She propped her

hands on her narrow hips. "That's not the point and you know it. I heard about the mess you made last night. I'm not in the mood to clean up after you two, and that's exactly what Nic's punishment will be if I let you in that room."

He could get in before she could stop him. They might grapple a bit, but eventually he'd topple her. Then he'd be through the door and—

No. It was too big of a risk for too little a reward. Amarante was just as likely to kick his ass today as she had been last night, probably more so. And if she made a stink about it, news would get back to Zhao and he'd be fucked. *Damn it.*

Tristan held up his hands. "I'll be good."

"And I'll believe that when I see it."

He didn't get a chance to move. The door opened and Amarante stood there. She didn't seem any different than she had during the meeting, cool and disinterested and so beautiful it hurt to look at her, just a little. She swept a look over him. "It's fine, Nari."

"Ms. Death—"

"We'll be on our best behavior."

Nari looked between them and cursed. "Understand that I'm calling this in and that you'll be watched for the duration of your conversation."

"Naturally." Amarante didn't look away from Tristan as she moved back a step and then another. Allowing him into the room. He wasted no time following her and closing the door behind him. A quick look around found two cameras perching in opposite corners of the room. There would be mics somewhere, but that was the rule when it came to the Warren. Every move was watched. Every word was listened to. The room itself was a board room nearly identical to the one they'd left a little while ago; a table dominating the middle of the room with a handful of chairs on either side.

Amarante didn't retreat to put the table between them, but he should have known she wouldn't. She just leaned back against it and watched him. "Did you know he was taking this angle?"

"No." No reason to lie. It wouldn't serve a purpose and, frankly, he was fucking pissed by the whole situation.

She gave a soft laugh. "I don't know why I ask. You won't tell me the truth."

"You're one to talk about *honesty*, Te." He should have kept his shit locked down, but all he could hear were Zhao's words echoing through his head. *She's not meant for you.*

Amarante was too good for him. He knew that, had known from the moment he met her that she stood on a pedestal above the rest of the world. Tristan didn't give a fuck if he didn't deserve her. They were two kindred souls and they both recognized it as idiot kids. Life had just gotten twisted up in the meantime. That didn't mean he was going to set aside everything he wanted simply because Zhao had finally decided to realize what a treasure his daughter was.

She didn't look away, but then Amarante never met a challenge she wouldn't rise to. "Shall we do this, then? You've obviously been chewing on it for the last ten years."

"You left me." The words felt torn from his chest. Too honest. He was never this fucking honest. "Your brother finally leveled up enough to get the money you wanted and you walked the fuck away from me without looking back."

She didn't blink. "It's interesting how you rewrite history."

There was no rewriting the feeling of her ripping his still-beating heart from his chest and taking it with her when she left. Tristan had never had a chance at normal. Normal wasn't for people like them. Worrying about colleges and mortgages and bills? What did that shit matter when they'd fought their way back from the brink of death time and time again before they turned eighteen? "You left."

"You took a job with *my father*."

"It was always meant to be temporary. I came back and you'd already cleared out."

She shook her head slowly. "Of course I left."

"I didn't know he was the one behind Camp Bueller." Not until a few months ago, and he still hadn't figured out what to do with the information when Zhao sent him after Ryu.

"Maybe not at first." She sliced her hand through the air. "But you knew who he was to me."

"Christ, Te, what do you want me to say? You weren't going to take me with you when you hit your big break. You know it and I know it. You were too busy taking care of your precious siblings."

Her eyes flashed. "We're not talking about them."

"The fuck we aren't. They were the albatross around your neck then, and they are now, too."

She shoved off the table. "Some of us understand loyalty, Tristan. Some of us know that you can't just cut a person loose because they might not be worth the investment. *Some* of us understand love."

"I understand love, Te."

"No, you fucking don't." She seemed to realize her volume had gotten away with her and tried to dial it back. "Love means sacrifice and loyalty and a whole list of traits you don't have. You're a monster, Tristan."

"That makes two of us."

She opened her mouth but seemed to reconsider what she'd been about to say. Her shoulders dropped a fraction of an inch before she reclaimed her position leaning against the table. "That makes two of us," she confirmed.

He hated that she acted like it was a bad thing, when being a monster was the only thing that made them willing to do what it took to stay alive. "They never appreciated what it took to survive; not like you did. They sure as shit don't appreciate what you did for them." He moved forward, unable to resist the pull of her. "What you're still doing for them. That's why you're here, isn't it? Sacrifice yourself so those assholes can ride off into the sunset together with fewer scars on their souls."

Amarante lifted her chin. "Someone has to bear the burden. Better me than anyone else."

He wanted to shake her, to shove the knowledge of her worth into her head once and for all. She'd always had skewed priorities. "You're worth ten times any of them."

"Tristan…" She shook her head. "You can't honestly think this is going to work. He offers the sweet and you come in with the sour, and between the two of you, you prod me into playing the part of obedient daughter."

Tristan should let her keep believing that. It would protect himself and probably protect her in the bargain. He'd never been one for lying, though. Not with this woman. "I stopped being here for him the second you told me to kiss you."

"If you say so."

He reached out but Amarante grabbed his wrist before his fingers made contact with her hair. She gave him a sharp smile. "I can't be accountable for what happens if you touch me."

"I'll take my chances." He pushed forward, all too aware that she allowed it, and sank his hands into her hair at the base of her skull. Tristan took the last step to bring them flush together. Fuck, she felt good. Lean and strong and dangerous in a way that had his cock going hard. "I missed you, Te."

"Stop saying that," she whispered.

"It's the truth."

Amarante kissed him. He knew beyond a shadow of a doubt that she only did it to shut him up, but Tristan was willing to play dirty. He'd keep talking until she silenced him over and over again, until they ground down the walls time and betrayal had built between them.

He drowned in the taste of her, knowing this could end at any moment. Amarante fisted her hands in his shirt, pulling him closer yet. She nipped his bottom lip, the sharp bite of pain only driving the pleasure of being this close to her higher. He tugged on her hair, tilting her face up to allow him to deepen the kiss. He wanted to keep kissing her forever, until the world fell away and Zhao disappeared and she stopped worrying so fucking much about a trio of adults who could take care of themselves. Until all she knew was him.

Tristan wasn't a romantic man. Wining and dining and pretty words were all just a different kind of lying, and he saw no benefit in stringing willing partners along. If he had a heart, it beat for one woman alone. He just never thought he'd get this close to her again.

Her hands fell to his pants, and he suddenly knew beyond a shadow of a doubt that if he fucked her on this table it would rock both their worlds right down to the core. Afterward, she'd shut him out. For good this time. Amarante could abide by no weakness, and letting him close enough to strike reeked of weakness. She'd assume Zhao would take advantage of it, would use her soft feelings for Tristan to attempt to manipulate her into doing what he wanted. She knew better than to make that mistake.

He wouldn't give her time to close the door on them completely.

Tristan pulled away. Amarante barely got a sound of protest out before he flipped her around and planted her hands on the table. "Not yet."

"If you don't—"

"Shhh." He undid the front of her slacks. "Let me take the edge off."

Her breath hissed out and she arched her hips, but he knew better than to overwhelm her completely. She cursed. "Either touch me or take off your pants."

"I'm going to touch you, Te." He had to close his eyes to keep control as he slipped a hand beneath her lace panties. Wet. She was so fucking wet just from that kiss. He traced her opening with a single finger. "Let me in."

She widened her stance, and he thanked whatever had caused her to decide on loose fitting pants today. Tristan planted his free hand next to hers on the table and pressed himself against the back of her body. Their layers of clothing had felt like too much when her mouth was on his, but now he wasn't sure if it would be enough to keep him on the straight and narrow.

Play the long game, asshole. A little pain now; a whole lot of pleasure later.

He slid a single finger into her and cursed. "Fuck, Te. You're so goddamn tight." Just pumping his finger slowly into her was enough to have him flashing back to that first night they spent together, when their friendship had crossed the line into something else. Fumbling in the dark like the pair of virgins they were. All awkward enthusiasm and whispered words he couldn't handle thinking about, even now.

Promises neither one of them kept.

He worked a second finger into her. The desire to tease this out, to keep her poised on the edge for as long as he could so this wouldn't end, nearly overwhelmed him. He pressed the heel of his hand against her clit. "I've got you."

"No, you don't." Her hips bucked and a ragged cry slipped from her lips as she ground down on his hand, fucking his fingers. He tried to pull back but it was too late. Amarante came with a soft sound that was almost a sob. Her knees buckled, and he barely caught her around the waist in time to keep her off the floor.

Even knowing better, Tristan set her on the table and kissed her again. She allowed it for one second, two, three. On the fourth, she gently pushed him away. "This was a mistake."

"No, it wasn't."

Amarante moved off the table and wobbled a little bit, but the scathing look she sent his way kept him from trying to touch her again. She fastened her pants quickly. "If he thinks this will smooth the way and make me more agreeable, he's picked the wrong angle."

He gritted his teeth, hating that she threw her father between them like a bomb. "He doesn't know I'm here."

"Tristan." She looked away and then back at him. "Respect me enough not to lie to me. You are his man, through and through. You know it. I know it. You do nothing without his command."

It was tempting to tell her exactly what would happen to him if Zhao found out about this little interlude, about Tristan's plans for Amarante. He knew better, though. Either she wouldn't believe him, or she'd use that information to further her own goals for being here. Amarante might be Tristan's priority at this point, but he knew better than to expect the same from her.

He'd always come second to her.

He cleared his throat and adjusted his cock in his pants. "What you're4 planning won't work. Zhao is too well protected."

Amarante smoothed her hair back into place. If not for the flush staining her cheeks, he'd almost be able to believe that she hadn't just come apart in his arms. She moved to the door. "I don't know what you're talking about."

Yes, she did. But he dropped it all the same. "Te."

She stopped with her hand on the doorknob. "Yes?"

"No matter what you think, it's not over between us."

"Yes, Tristan. It is." She walked out the door without looking back.

CHAPTER 7

*A*marante barely kept it together long enough to make it back to her room. She half expected Tristan to follow, had almost relished the idea of going another round with him. Fighting or fucking. That kind of thing was more up her sister's alley than Amarante's. She didn't lose control. She couldn't afford to, not with all the responsibilities weighing on her shoulders.

From the moment she and her siblings purchased the Island of Ys and built the resort from the ground up, she'd known that hers was not a position that meant giving in to impulses. Too much rode on her words and actions. Over the years, there had been plenty of men—and no small number of women—who looked at Death and thought a place in her bed would secure them the kind of power they craved. She never took any of them up on their offers. She couldn't afford for them to be right, for their presence and the potential pleasure they offered to cloud her mind, to muddy her plan.

Cora was the only exception, but she'd long since proven that she had no interest in the Horsemen outside of

Amarante's friendship. Just like Amarante had proven that she enjoyed Cora's company, not her identity as Lust, one of the Virtuous Sins. Even then, they held themselves at a certain distance.

Less than twenty-four hours in the Warren and she had to admit that her paranoia that kept everyone away had a basis in truth. Two kisses. One orgasm. That was all it took for her to start softening toward Tristan. For her to start *craving* him.

She hadn't wanted to stop. Not last night and not today. She couldn't trust herself around him, and that was a massive complication because if the meeting today was any indication, Zhao intended to keep his right-hand man close. Maybe this whole thing really *was* part of the underhanded negotiations. She couldn't be sure, couldn't afford to take anything for granted.

Amarante walked to the table that held the phone and stared at it. Calling Kenzie right now would be a mistake, but for the first time in years, she didn't know what to do. She'd have an easier time if Tristan was attempting to kill her. *That* Amarante knew how to deal with. But his overwhelming words and the way he touched her, kissed her, made her come? No, she had no framework for this.

She never expected to come face to face with him again. Not really. They parted ways on poor terms, and Amarante had no interest in her father before discovering that he was the one who funded and ran Camp Bueller. No doubt he had some other *camp* set up even now since Bueller was abandoned sometime after Amarante and her siblings escaped it. Zhao was evil in human form.

She was Death.

One breath. Another. Another. Inhale and exhale until her thoughts stopped their frantic circling. She could handle anything he threw at her. She already had. This thing with

Tristan was no different. It was simply a matter of approaching things from a logical perspective. Line up the evidence, consider her options, and then act decisively.

First, she needed more information.

With that decided, Amarante didn't hesitate to pick up the phone. She dialed Kenzie's number and listened to it ring. Her sister hadn't gotten many words in edgewise on the last call, but without their brothers interrupting, no doubt she'd have plenty to say. Best to let her get it out and then cut through the rage with a few cold words.

But when Kenzie answered, she sounded calm and pleasant. "You know, you've really pissed off a lot of people with this little stunt, Amarante."

Flying to certain death was hardly a *stunt*, especially when done to protect them, but she clenched her jaw and kept the comment internal. "I need your help."

A significant pause. "Why do I suspect that you're not calling to request my delightful presence to back you up?"

"Because I'm not." Having her siblings in the Warren would just give Zhao more targets. If he truly wanted her back in the fold, he wouldn't hesitate to remove Luca and Kenzie. They weren't blood, and that was obviously all that mattered to Zhao if he thought something as mundane as genetic ties would cause her to forgive and forget all his many sins.

More, if Amarante managed to complete her goal in killing him, she would be the only one here to suffer the consequences. The reason the Warren was so effective, beyond the obvious, was because a breaking of the rules went all the way to the top. If one of your staff broke the rules, the person they answered to was punished as well as the person *they* answered to, assuming they were on the property. Nicholai and his people were unrelenting, which meant they didn't have to enact that threat often. If the others were here when she acted, there was a very large chance they would see the same consequences she would.

She had no intention of dying, but she couldn't risk their lives on her gamble.

Finally, Kenzie sighed. "Luca and Ryu are half a second from planning an assault on the Warren. You could have played this a hundred different ways, all of which were better options."

"No, I couldn't." Not with the time she had, not with the threat rising against them the closer they came to the truth. Amarante replayed Kenzie's words in her head. "You're not participating in the plans?"

"Why did you call?"

She could press, could ask what Kenzie was avoiding telling her, but digging the truth out of her sister before Kenzie was ready to talk represented an impossible task. "I... need some advice." Her sister gasped and she straightened. "What's wrong?"

"The honorable Amarante needs advice? I'm shocked. Shocked, I tell you."

She closed her eyes and tried to exhale through the adrenaline surge. Damn it, she should have known Kenzie would play this up for all it was worth. She *would* have known if she was thinking clearly. "Get it all out of your system now so you can focus."

"Oh, I'm focused like a laser. What's this about? You've never come to me for advice before."

"Yes, I have."

Kenzie laughed a little. "No, Te, you haven't. We might plan together as a group, but you always plot your own course and the rest of us fall into line because you're brilliant and most of the time you're right. Not this time, of course, but I'd be lying if I said your track record was anything less than stellar."

That warmed her while simultaneously making her feel like shit. Life was complicated. "I value your opinions. All of you."

"I never said you didn't. You just steamroll right over us when it suits you." Kenzie cleared her throat. "Look, I'm not trying to read you the riot act. We're in this place because you're a badass bitch who will cut her way through anything that rises up against us, and you taught us to survive. I'm still going to kick your ass for pulling this bullshit, but I'm not surprised by it the same way the boys are. If I'd been thinking clearly when all the stuff with Ryu went down, I would have realized this would be your play."

Amarante wouldn't apologize for doing what needed to be done. Not even to Kenzie. Not when it would keep them safe from the thing that haunted their shared past. Vengeance and justice may be two sides to the same coin, but they both demanded the same price.

Zhao's head on a platter, his empire burned to ash and scattered to the wind.

She had the strongest urge to hang up and end this conversation before she admitted how far out of her control this situation had become. Amarante muscled down the impulse. She was as good as she was because she knew her limits. This thing with Tristan was a limit, a blind spot she couldn't afford to ignore. "I have a problem."

"A problem I can help you with. I got it. Stop stalling and tell me what's going on."

She took a deep breath. "Do you remember the first few years when we were in the city after we got out?" No need to name the place they escaped. "All those times I disappeared?"

"Sure. Most of the time you came back with food or whatever we needed."

Yes, because Tristan had taught her how to pick pockets and a hundred little tricks to make people ignore her so she could do what it took to survive. She pressed her lips together. Admitting this felt like admitting a deep, dark sin, but Kenzie couldn't give her the appropriate advice without all the information. "I met someone. He helped me, helped us. We were... friends."

Silence for several long moments. "Okay," Kenzie said slowly. "This is a weird secret and also feels really big. Why didn't you tell us?"

"Because he was mine. He made me feel... not normal, exactly, but as close as I had ever come to it." Selfish, maybe, but she'd spent so many years committing acts no child should know about, let alone participate in. And when they finally escaped, she had the others to care for. Luca had only been twelve, and Kenzie not much older. At seventeen, Amarante was not prepared for the realities of flying below the radar and staying alive. Tristan had helped.

"I get that in a weird way, I guess." A sound like she gave herself a shake. "Okay, so this guy was a friend and helped you."

To tell the rest or not? She shook her head. She'd gone too far to back out now. "We were friends, and then we were more."

Kenzie's shocked gasp nearly made her laugh. Her sister recovered fast, though. "Does anyone else know about this?"

"I think Luca suspects that there was something else going on." He'd found her right after Tristan had left for good, when the weight of the future had taken her to her knees. Neither of them had spoken about it since. "But no, not really."

"Wait a minute, why are you telling me about this now?" She didn't give her a chance to answer, barreling on in the way that only Kenzie could. "Holy shit, is it Nicholai?"

"What? No. *No.*" She braced herself. "It's Tristan. Zhao Fai's right hand man."

Silence for a beat. Two. "No fucking shit?" Kenzie whispered. "What are the odds of that?"

She'd had weeks to think about it since discovering the identity of the mystery person they'd spent so much of their lives hunting. Since realizing *her father* was responsible. "Pretty good considering I don't think Zhao ever lost track of us." She hadn't thought too much about the coincidence of Tristan getting placement with her father at the time, had been too caught up in the betrayal of his choice and then in pursuing her own goals while determined not to think about him.

"He snatched up the guy you had feelings for." Kenzie still sounded shell-shocked. "I mean, it's barely a blip on the evil scale considering the other shit he's responsible for, but that's still fucked up."

"Yes."

"And now Tristan is part of said evil empire. Fuck, Te, that's *really* shitty. I'm sorry."

If only it ended there. She swallowed hard. "He's here. Tristan."

"Of course he is. It's a brilliant play to undermine you, trotting out the guy you had feelings for that he stole. He should know better, though."

She appreciated Kenzie's faith in her, even if it was misplaced. "I wasn't prepared. I thought I was, but he's already making me crazy. Every time I turn around, he's there and it feels like he's beneath my skin. I... Kenzie, I'm losing control."

"You've only been there like twenty-four hours."

"That's exactly my point." She couldn't make herself get into the details of what happened a short time ago in that board room, not when her body still felt pliant and buzzed from the orgasm. Pliant and buzzed and aching for more. "I'm not certain I can hold out indefinitely."

Just like that, the shock was gone from Kenzie's voice and she was all business. "Have you kissed him?"

"Yes."

"More?"

"Yes." It felt like setting down a burden she'd carried for days to admit as much. She leaned against the table and took a slow breath. "I want more."

"Of course you want more. I would say fuck someone else immediately, but we both know you won't. Even your thing with Cora is too controlled to hold up against what he's bringing to the table."

The thought of having sex with someone else—even Cora —didn't hold a candle to the temptation Tristan offered . She closed her eyes. "I don't understand why it's him."

"Honey, it sounds like he was really, really important to you at one point. You aren't a person who can just turn something like that off, no matter how many years you spent apart. Unresolved feelings only get more complicated with time. Ask me how I know." Kenzie had just dealt with a vaguely similar situation when her one night stand from years before showed up and refused to leave until she gave him a chance. That had worked out, but it didn't mean a damn thing. Liam wasn't working for the enemy. He hasn't chosen the enemy over Kenzie. "We don't get a choice in who we respond to." Kenzie cleared her throat. "How can I help?"

Even talking this much has helped. Not with a plan for the future, but to let her draw in her first full breath since she walked into the Warren and saw Tristan. "I can't control myself when I'm around him."

"Okay, two questions."

She braced herself. "All right."

"Do your feelings for Tristan affect how you plan to move forward with Zhao?"

That was easy. "No. Not in the least." She would not be turned from her course of action.

"Second question; would he hurt you if you let him close?"

Amarante blinked. "Do you mean physically or otherwise?"

"Either. Both."

She took her time in answering. "Not physically. We did get... heated... last night, but it was a mutual thing. But no, he's had several chances to get beneath my guard and harm me and hasn't."

Kenzie let that sit for a moment. "And emotionally?"

"I don't know." She wished she could say it wouldn't hurt her to let him close even physically and then have him walk away again, but Amarante tried not to lie to herself. She couldn't guarantee her reaction, just like she couldn't guarantee what the future held at this point. "It's entirely possible."

"I don't think you can scratch the itch and walk away, Te. You're not really built like that." Kenzie exhaled. "But don't beat yourself up if you make that call. You're human, and you're doing the best you can."

The best she could.

Right.

She just hoped it was good enough.

CHAPTER 8

Zhao took one look at Tristan's face the next morning and banished him from the morning talks. As much as sitting in a room while they verbally circled and swiped at each other sounded like a little sliver of hell, Tristan resented the shit out of Zhao for keeping him from the one person in this godforsaken building he actually wanted to see.

He knew better than to cross the old man, though.

Instead, he stalked the hallways of the Warren. He wasn't even particularly surprised to turn a corner and find Nic leaning against the wall. The man pushed off it and nodded. "You're making my people nervous."

"Maybe they should be nervous." He sure as fuck felt like he was going out of his skin. Being so close to Amarante and not able to close that last bit of distance was driving him mad. It wasn't just the fucking, though he'd be lying if he said the fucking wasn't part of it. No, he just flat out missed her.

Nic shook his head. "Come on. They'll be busy for a few more hours."

He fell into step next to his friend. Tristan didn't like that many people, but he'd felt that instant kinship with Nic that he felt when he met Amarante all those years ago. With one marked difference. He didn't want to get into Nic's pants.

They'd met when Zhao sent Tristan to the Warren to broker a small deal with an enemy that had become a nuisance. Negotiations ended early and Tristan had spent the rest of the week bullshitting with Nic. Since then, he made sure he visited quarterly for a day or two.

"You want to talk about it?"

He didn't look over. "Nothing to talk about."

"You sure?" Nic pushed open a door and into a secondary set of hallways. They looked indistinguishable from the one they just left, but Tristan knew better. They were in the part of the Warren meant for Nic's people alone. The reaction in his friend was a small but notable relaxing of his shoulders. He glanced at Tristan. "You're wound so tight, you're practically a walking thundercloud. Dial it back."

That was the problem. If he could dial it back, he would have already, and he'd be sitting across the table from Amarante instead of walking *here*. "She's not safe with Zhao."

Nic snorted. "No shit, she's not safe with Zhao. That's the whole purpose of having their meetings here instead of somewhere else. Nari is one of my best. She'll take care of your girl."

"She's not my girl." Not anymore. Maybe not ever. He wasn't sure. They'd never had to put a label on what they were, because what they were surpassed labels.

"Sure. Whatever you have to tell yourself." He snorted. "I've never seen you like this."

"That's because I've never *been* like this." He didn't feel like getting into the emotional bullshit of it. Nic was his friend, but he was still the ruler of the Warren, and that meant if it came down to a choice between preserving the Warren's reputation and Tristan, he'd cut off Tristan's head without hesitation. He'd feel bad about it afterward, but he'd do it.

He dragged his hands through his hair. "You're sure she's safe."

"I'm going to pretend you didn't ask me that so we can still be friends." Nic slipped his hands into his pockets, his expression carefully blank. "She's sitting in a room with *your* boss, Tristan. You taking a minute to stop and think about those implications? You that worried about him, why are you working with him?"

Tristan gave him the look that comment deserved. "Right. Because you were so fond of the last guy who ran the Warren."

Nic held up his hands. "It's a valid question. You feel this strongly about this woman, maybe working for her sworn enemy isn't the right call. Maybe it never was."

He wanted to snap back that Nic didn't know what the fuck he was talking about, but they were too good of friends for it to be anything but a lie. Tristan picked up his pace even though they weren't actually going anywhere, just wandering these halls to burn off some of his excess energy. "I was young when he got me. He offered me everything I wanted—a chance at money. A chance at *power*. I went from being a homeless pickpocket to having more money than I knew what to do with."

"You had to know it wasn't on the up and up."

He snorted. "No shit, it wasn't on the up and up." Not the jobs Zhao sent him on, and not the old man's reason for pulling him in. It took him too long to figure it out, but he'd been so consumed with climbing the ranks and putting as much money and power between him and the boy he'd been that there hadn't been much room for reflection.

Losing Amarante shocked him down to his core, but by then it was too late. She was gone and he had exactly one thing going for him. He'd made it to the top in record time because he didn't have the same hang ups that other guys did. When a person had already lost the only thing they cared about, it made everything else a lot clearer.

Plus, he lacked anything resembling a conscience. That helped, too.

Nic finally sighed. "You're not going to settle down until you know she's fine."

"Pretty much."

"You do realize you're talking about *Death*, right? In a fight between her and Zhao, I'd have to think long and hard about placing my bets."

Yeah, Tristan, too. In a fair fight, she'd win. But Zhao never fought fair, and he never even stepped onto the battle-field unless he was sure of his win.

He hadn't come to the Warren to lose.

"You know, I had shit to do today that didn't involve babysitting your ass."

"Then go do it. I'll handle myself."

"That's what I'm afraid of." Nic shook his head. "Come on." He led the way through a series of turns before opening a door that looked like every other one Tristan had walked past this morning. This one led to a short hallway with a locked door at the other end of it. Nic pressed his hand to the screen next to the door and the lock clicked open. "Try not to piss any of my people off."

"Who, me?" He put on his most charming smile. "Everyone loves me."

"I'd venture to say a good half of our world wants to stab you in the throat."

"Like I said—everyone loves me." He followed Nic through the door.

The Warren more than earned its name with its public hallways and rooms tucked away in unexpected places. Most of the guests never saw this side of the place. Not unless they'd fucked up so badly, Nic had to step in. In which case, they never lived to speak of it.

The staff hallways were mostly straight, which amused Tristan to no end. He followed Nic to one of the many surveillance rooms littered throughout the building. It wasn't the main security room, of course; no matter how good of friends, Nic would never allow him access *there*.

After shutting the door, Nic keyed up the computer and pointed at the chair. "Sit."

"Woof."

"Asshole."

He dropped into the chair and watched Nic key in the password to get the system up and running. His fingers moved too fast for Tristan to track, but he wasn't really trying. Their friendship was built on a fragile sort of trust. Tristan could answer Zhao's questions honestly if he intentionally didn't collect information while he was here visiting.

Better for everyone that way.

He didn't *think* Zhao would move against the Warren. To do so and fail was a death sentence. To do it and succeed... He didn't know what that would look like. It would rock their shadowy world to its core, and that wasn't good for business, no matter what Zhao planned. The Warren only worked because everyone feared it equally. If they thought for a second that Nic was killable, or that the rules could be bent, they'd eat everyone in this building alive.

The screen cleared to show the same boardroom they'd been in the day before. Nari stood behind Amarante, and Lennox leaned against the wall behind Zhao. Amarante held herself perfectly straight in her seat, clothed today in another suit that would have been far too formal if a man was wearing it. Somehow, she pulled it off. She always did, though.

71

Zhao looked the same as ever. Crafty and in control and toying with his prey.

"Do we have sound?"

Nic snorted. "Of course we have sound. What kind of operation do you think I'm running here?" He clicked a button and Te and Zhao's voices filtered through the speaker.

Zhao leaned forward. "You know, it's rather telling that you choose that style. If you were more secure in your power, you'd dress like a woman."

Nic made a choked sound. "That's one kind of strategy."

"Yeah." Tristan leaned forward and frowned at the screen. Zhao wasn't stupid. He had to know that this was a long shot under the best of circumstances, let alone if he was intent on pissing Amarante off during every meeting. Tristan had watched him skillfully manipulate those around him to get the end result he wanted. Which suggested that his stated goal might not be the real one.

Tristan clenched his jaw. "Can you turn this up?"

"Sure." Nic hit a few more buttons.

Amarante didn't so much as twitch. She stared coolly at her father. "You have a strange way of negotiating. Do you often talk like this to the other party, or am I special because I'm a woman?"

"You're my daughter."

That got a reaction, albeit a tiny one. Her shoulders went tight. "I have no mother. I certainly have no father."

"You're too old for teenage rebellion."

Tristan thought that would break through her cool exterior. Amarante was only a teen—something like fifteen—when she earned the nickname Little Death in that camp. Zhao had to know that.

Then again, Tristan had long since given up trying to read the old man's mind. He didn't think Zhao would have thrown his only two children into hell and walked away without looking back, but he couldn't fathom a logical reason why Zhao would have sent them there in the first place. Tristan was cold as shit, but they were just *kids*. Amarante was *seven* at the time.

"Easy," Nic murmured.

He realized he'd fisted his hands at his sides and made himself relax. None of this information was new. She'd told him herself when they were friends all those years ago. Tristan had been shocked to discover the Horsemen were coming for Zhao, had been shocked to find out Zhao was behind Camp Bueller... until he'd really thought about it.

Zhao was responsible for all sorts of bad shit out in the world. Was it really surprising he'd stoop to Bueller levels? No.

It still didn't explain sending his own flesh and blood there. If it was meant to be a proving ground the way he claimed, he should have scooped them up the second they escaped.

None of this lined up.

Amarante tapped her finger against the table. "You're wasting both our time." She looked at Zhao. Nothing showed on her face. No hurt, no irritation, no recognition at all. She'd bottled it all up. "You have only a couple days left of this summit. If you plan to spend it like you did yesterday, then I see no reason to stay."

"Threats, Amarante?" Zhao gave a dry chuckle. "We both know you're not walking out of here before the end of this."

"Do we?"

"How can you expect to kill me if you turn tail and run at the first hiccup in your plan?"

She didn't so much as react. "Murder on Warren property carries a significant punishment. I prefer my skin intact."

"Ah, but you finally have your white whale. How long have you spent hunting me, even before you knew it was me?" Zhao still had the amused paternal expression on his face. "Your whole life. A quarter of a century wanting my head as punishment. What's your life in compared with that kind of vengeance?"

That got the tiniest reaction. A tiny dip at the edges of her lips. Not a frown, but a reaction all the same. "I value my life more highly than that."

"Without a doubt." But Zhao had her exactly where he wanted her. He appeared too pleased for it to be anything but the truth. "But we're not just talking about you, are we? There are three other Horsemen. And they've all acquired significant others, which we both know only translates to significant blind spots. Your ship is full of holes, daughter. It's going down. There's only one way to ensure all those soft, vulnerable spots remain safe, and that's to remove me."

"You're making an excellent case for your death." Amarante still hadn't moved, still hadn't stopped the slow and steady tapping of her finger. "It's enough to make one wonder your motivation. Are you tired of living, Zhao? You're an old man, after all. It's been known to happen." Tap. Tap. Tap. "If you're interested in death by enemy, there are better ways to go about it."

His mouth went tight, but almost instantly relaxed into a smile. "That was a well-placed barb."

Nic hit the mute button. "I'm aware of your allegiance to Zhao."

It took Tristan a few beats longer to tear his attention from the screen. Amarante was fine. She had *been* fine this whole time; she didn't need him to protect her. But then, she never had.

He turned to Nic. "You have a reason for asking that question that isn't a question."

"If he attempts to break the neutral ground of the Warren, he *will* be punished. I don't give a fuck who he is or how powerful he is outside these walls." He stared hard at Tristan. "And if he commands you to do it, I'll do the same to you, Tristan. We're friends, but some things go beyond friendship."

"I'm aware." He glanced at the screen and made himself turn away. "I don't know what his plan is." That, in and of itself, wasn't completely unusual. Zhao liked to play his cards close to his chest. But he tended to loop Tristan in on important shit—and this farce of a summit was *important* shit.

Nic's green eyes turned speculative. "That's rather telling, isn't it?"

"Yeah. I guess it is."

CHAPTER 9

*E*very word out of Zhao's mouth pricked at Amarante, poking and prodding and attempting to get a reaction. To what end, she had no idea. She'd come in expecting threats and a demand that she cease and desist in her systematic attacks against those beneath Zhao.

None of this had gone like she'd planned.

Zhao sat back and folded his hands over his stomach. "Come back to me and I'll declare that little island of yours to be untouchable."

She might have laughed if she wasn't doing everything in her power not to leap across the table and stab him in the neck with her pen. Even without Tristan in the room, Nicholai's people would ensure she didn't succeed. "My island *is* untouchable."

His grin widened. "Is it, daughter?"

The small hairs at the nape of her neck stood on end. "You know that old saying about honey and vinegar? Threatening my home is not the way to go bringing me around to your way of thinking."

"I think we both know that you're not going to be *brought around* without some heavy-handedness on my part. Unfortunate, that." He shrugged. "But a father does what he must."

Rage rose in a tidal wave. She took a careful breath. Losing it now was out of the question. If he knew just how thoroughly he'd wormed his way beneath her skin, he'd go in for the kill. She still didn't know what he wanted, either. Taking his offer at face value...

She wasn't foolish enough to do so.

His threats, on the other hand, were something else altogether. "If you do anything to threaten my home or my family, it will be perceived as an act of war. There will be no need for this farce of a summit then, because there will be nothing left to say."

Zhao held up his hands, still seeming amused. "I was simply thinking out loud. An island is so vulnerable in so many ways. I know it matters to you."

A threat made with a smile was no less a threat. Amarante tilted her head to the side. "So what you're saying is that you will leave what's mine alone if I do as you demand. Interesting, considering if I join your operations, what's mine becomes yours." She would never join him. He was too smart to believe otherwise.

But then, smart men had been brought down by their own visions before. It was possible *she* was Zhao's blind spot.

She didn't think so, though.

Amarante had never had a problem looking at the playing field and knowing exactly what everyone on it would do before they did it. People were ultimately exactly as they appeared to be. Occasionally, they surprised her a little, but when push came to shove, everyone reverted to their base nature.

Zhao, on the other hand, defied understanding. She didn't

know why he'd sent her and Ryu away. She didn't know why he'd come to her like this now, rather than treating her as the enemy she was. What she didn't know could get her killed and see him walk free. Unacceptable. She had to be better than this. She was letting him get to her.

"Zhao Fai. Father." She nearly choked on the word. "We can circle and beat our chests for the next few days, or you can provide a show of good faith to prove you mean exactly what you say." She wouldn't believe it for a moment, but she needed more information.

"I'm listening."

Keeping her voice even and disinterested took more effort than it should have. "Camp Bueller was the only place of that nature that you presided over."

Zhao's expression didn't change. "It was, yes."

She pressed on. "When it closed, you moved operations. I want to know where."

He boomed out a laugh. "I know how this goes, daughter. I indulge this line of questioning, and within a few days, the full fury of the Horsemen of Ys comes down on a place of business that I own."

He'd as much as admitted that there was another camp. Another location of torture and horror where *children* were being victimized. Amarante didn't blink. "Surely a prominent business man like yourself doesn't need that kind of location to gain profit. Really, Zhao, it's crass."

"Crass." He smiled at her. "You know how these things work. Many arms, many incomes, all for the sake of stability. Providing certain people with certain tastes is simply good business."

Simply. Good. Business.

Amarante had crossed so many lines over the years, she barely had a single boundary left. With her back against the wall and her siblings looking to her to lead them, there hadn't been time to be precious about survival. Later, when the number of those under her care grew as the Island of Ys grew, the responsibility had required her to make hard choices again and again. She never let anyone know the cost. It was hers to bear, and hers alone.

Yet one thing remained sacred.

Children.

Zhao had to know that. It was why he subtly taunted her with this talk of *certain tastes* as if hurting children was in line with enjoying seafood. Amarante stared him down, not giving him the satisfaction of a reaction. "I suppose it's up to you to decide what my presence is worth." She pushed slowly to her feet. "I think we're done here."

"You're playing a dangerous game, daughter."

Daughter. Over and over again, he drove the reminder of their blood relation home. Whether he did it to harm or in an attempt to bridge the gap between them was anyone's guess. Amarante didn't care. She turned for the door.

"Wait."

She stopped, her hand on the doorknob. "Yes?"

"It's a few hours north of Hazelton."

She closed her eyes for several long beats. They hadn't moved to another country, another part of the world. They'd moved that fucking camp a half day's drive from the old one. Amarante opened her eyes. Whipping herself for the oversight could be done later. Right now, she had to get out of here before she forgot herself and went after him. She could almost feel the pain sparking along her fist as she beat his smug fucking face in, the give of his nose beneath her blows. She wouldn't stop until he was unrecognizable.

Amarante turned the knob and walked out of the room. Nari's heels clipped behind her, but she didn't look over her shoulder at the other woman. Not when she knew her reaction was written all over her face for anyone to see.

She strode down the hallway in the direction of the elevator. The obvious thing to do was to tell her siblings the location of the base and let them take care of it. Or at least begin the process to take care of it. Even if she didn't survive this summit, they would ensure that the children captive in that place were rescued and taken care of.

It could be a trap.

No, it *was* a trap.

Zhao wouldn't give that information without an ulterior motive, no matter how much he claimed to want her to take this theoretical role within his operation. Either he had lied about the location, or he wanted to use this move to eliminate the other Horsemen. They weren't operating at peak performance right now. Not with Luca still healing from several gunshot wounds and Ryu seven different kinds of distracted because of his new woman. And Kenzie? She'd just faced down her own personal demon not too long ago. Even if she seemed well enough, she couldn't be trusted to react rationally without someone there to check her.

They needed Amarante to pull this off, and she was the one thing they couldn't have.

She reached the elevator and it opened without hesitation. A quick scan and they were shooting upward to her floor. Nari wisely said nothing, which was just as well. This entire situation had gone from problematic to impossible and she still hadn't had a chance to get Zhao alone. At this point, her best bet was Tristan, and that wasn't a good plan by any stretch of the imagination. Getting close to him meant putting herself at risk. Maybe not necessarily physically, though she couldn't rule that out at this point.

Tristan got beneath her defenses too easily. He always had. Even Kenzie recognized it, because her suggestion to get "it" out of her system had been halfhearted at best. They both knew there was no getting something out of Amarante's system once it took up residence. When she cared for people, it wasn't something she could turn off.

It's why she went out of her way not to let anyone close.

If that was her goal, she was about ten years too late on it with Tristan.

Nari waited for her to open her door and gave a little wave. "Let me know if you're planning on leaving the room before tomorrow's meetings and I'll pop up here."

"I'm not."

"See you tomorrow, then."

Amarante shut the door carefully when all she wanted to do was slam it. The display of violence wouldn't help. Tearing through this room and destroying everything she could get her hands on wouldn't help, either. It'd feel good in the moment, but then she'd be left with the destruction. She didn't think Nicholai would report on the loss of control to Tristan—and through him, Zhao—but she couldn't be sure.

Because she couldn't be sure, she kicked off her heels and strode through the suite to the bedroom. She stripped in short, economical movements and padded naked into the bathroom. Only when the shower was going and she stood beneath the spray did she allow herself to react.

A sob ripped from her lips.

Amarante pressed both hands to her mouth, muffling the sound. She'd thought she was prepared for this. Really, she should have known better. There was no preparing for facing down the past, especially when the truths hidden there were so incredibly ugly. No amount of control would change them. Nothing she could do would change anything about the past.

There was only the future.

Time passed and eventually she was able to straighten and release a long exhale. There were still two days left of dealing with Zhao. Two days of trying to find a way to chop the head off the snake. It had seemed difficult, but not impossible when she agreed to attend this sham. Now, she wasn't so sure she could pull it off. There was no opportunity.

The plan needed to be adjusted.

She wrapped herself in one of the soft fluffy robes and walked back into the bedroom. The thought of getting dressed again, of stuffing all her emotions down deep so she could present a strong front long enough to get a meal... Amarante couldn't do it. Instead, she tightened the tie on the robe and moved to the living room. Pacing was more Kenzie's thing than hers, but her feet found a pattern and she walked it over and over again.

Calling her siblings was out of the question. Not without more of a plan, more of *something* to ensure they all walked out alive. Amarante stopped short. If she succeeded in killing Zhao here, the knowledge of the new camp would die with her when Nicholai enforced his laws. It wouldn't matter if the place was a trap because the other Horsemen would never know about it.

She closed her eyes and stood perfectly still. There was a way through this. She just had to *think*.

A knock on her door brought a curse to her lips. She marched there and yanked it open. Finding Tristan there didn't surprise her, not really. He had his hands in his pockets and a carefully blank expression on his face. "Can I come in?"

She looked behind him, even though she knew better. For all the Warren's so-called extreme security, Tristan certainly moved about wherever and whenever he wanted to. As tempting as it was to close the door in his face, she found herself stepping back and letting him into her room. It wasn't until she shut and locked the door behind him that she registered that Tristan was *in her room*.

Not to mention she wore nothing but a robe.

She started to cross her arms over her chest and abandoned the motion halfway through. "What do you want, Tristan?"

Though she expected him to respond with something irreverent, he moved to the faux window and stared into the night sky pictured there. "Something's wrong."

"You're going to have to be slightly more specific. Many things are wrong." Children trapped in a place designed to torture them for the pleasure of rich sociopaths. Her siblings in danger. Her plan in shambles.

Tristan turned back to her. "In all the time I've worked for Zhao, he's never operated like this. It's clumsy."

She couldn't argue that. Being forced to sit in a room with him, or engage in the planned activities, all while he badgered her from one direction and then another... She didn't believe for a second that he considered her life a proving ground of some unknown test, or that he would accept her as some prodigal daughter even if she was interested. A man like Zhao worked too hard for his power to share it, even with an heir. It wasn't how he functioned.

But she couldn't trust Tristan.

A small, weak part of her wanted his being here to be proof that he truly cared. That he was choosing *her* over Zhao instead of the other way around like he did all those years ago. Amarante straightened. Maybe *that* was the play. Zhao put her off her guard and Tristan moved in from the other side to angle for her weak spot. "You should leave."

"Te, you're not listening to me."

"I'm listening. To everything." That was the problem. She couldn't turn her head off. She'd never been able to, even when she was with him. Even as off-center as she felt right now, her mind was still spinning, spinning, spinning. "Why are you here, Tristan?"

His jaw tightened and he finally met her gaze. "I'm here for you, Te."

Words she desperately wanted to hear... ten years ago. Hearing them *now*, when she had so much at stake and he was the enemy? It felt like a slap in the face. Amarante strode to the door. "Get out. Get out right fucking now."

CHAPTER 10

*O*ne look at Amarante's face told Tristan that if he tried to argue, he'd have a literal fight on his hands. While the thought thrilled him on one level, it wasn't why he'd come here. He held up his hands slowly. "I'm going."

If eyes could shoot literal lasers, he'd be melted flesh and bone on the ground. Amarante grabbed the door knob and yanked it open. "Out!"

He barely had a moment to realize that the doorway wasn't empty. A white man stood there, dressed in the same color clothing as all Nic's staff. He had a tray in his hands and looked vaguely surprised to have the door open in his face. There wasn't a single thing about him that seemed suspicious except his presence itself. No reason for the hair at the back of Tristan's neck to stand on end.

He trusted his instincts, though, and his body reacted before his brain had a chance to catch up. He made it two huge steps closer before the man blinked and *changed*. It was a trick of posture, a straightening of his shoulders, a look in his nondescript brown eyes. "Death." He dropped the tray and a gun appeared in his hand.

"Te, *down*."

She reacted the instant the words left his mouth, ducking down to the floor as the man fired two bullets that would have taken her in the face. Tristan leapt over her and grabbed the assassin's arm, forcing it up and away from Amarante. Even though the guy was smaller than Tristan, he had a deceptive amount of muscle packed on his lean frame. He wrenched his arm free and lifted the gun again.

Shit.

A metal tray came flying past Tristan's shoulder and winged the man. He fell back a step, already lifting the gun again. Fuck, this guy was like the Terminator. They could take him out. Probably. But Tristan couldn't guarantee that they'd do it without injury. He could handle whatever this asshole dealt out. The thought of Amarante with a bullet hole, though? The very idea had him spinning around and shoving her back into the room. He slammed the door and flipped the deadbolt.

"What the hell are you doing?"

"These doors can damn near hold up against explosives. A bullet won't penetrate."

Amarante looked like she wanted to beam him in the head a few times with that metal tray. "He's going to escape."

"He's not going to escape. He's in the fucking Warren." He stalked to the phone. It started ringing before he had a chance to lift it. Tristan snatched it from its cradle. "You fucked up."

"Stay in the room. We're taking care of it. Under no circumstances are either of you to leave." Nic hung up.

Tristan snorted. "Fat chance of that."

"What was that?"

He opened his mouth, but the sound of Nic's voice filled the room. He suspected it filled the entire building. The tension in his friend's voice on the phone was nowhere in evidence now. "There is a small situation. My staff is taking care of it immediately, but all guests must remain in your room for the duration. To discourage anyone from getting foolish ideas, I've taken the liberty of engaging the locks. They will be released once the situation is resolved."

"No," Amarante murmured. "Absolutely not." She flipped the deadbolt and yanked on the door. Nothing happened. She cursed and yanked it again. It didn't so much as budge. "He can't just lock us in here."

"Apparently he can." Tristan hadn't even been aware that this was a feature the Warren had. In all his time moving through the shadows of this world, he'd never heard so much as a rumor of it being engaged. Which meant it likely hadn't.

Then again, the Warren had never been breached before, either.

"I can't do this."

It then that he realized her eyes were too wide. She was shaking. Holy shit, Amarante was about to lose it. Tristan almost went to her, but he couldn't guarantee that his proximity wouldn't set her off worse. "It'll be fine, Te. Just need to cool our heels for a bit and then I'll get out of your hair."

She gave him a long look and stalked into the bedroom. Tristan *definitely* knew better than to follow her there without an invitation. He could dance on the edge of being a dick, but Amarante would literally rip his balls off if he crossed the line. He was quite attached to that part of his anatomy, so he dropped into a chair and studied the suite.

Reinforced door. No windows out. Maximum security, just as the Warren promised. No one ever thought about how the rooms could quickly become jail cells. Nic and a selection of his people would have override codes, but if there was a fire… Yeah, there had to be another way out of this room.

A last resort to look into. Right now, Tristan was exactly where he wanted to be, even if Amarante wasn't interested in hearing him out. That was fine. He now had time to figure out how to make her listen.

She stalked back into the room with—

Tristan perked up. "Is that a joint?"

"That's a stupid question." She dropped into the chair across from him and flicked the lighter in her other hand. "We're going to be stuck here for who knows how long, and I have no interest in getting drunk with you in my room. This will take the edge off and keep me functioning." She lit the end of the joint and took a long inhale. "Stop looking at me like that."

"Te—"

"If you're about to tell me that fucking can take the edge off, I will hold you down and light *you* on fire."

Considering he'd been about to do exactly that, he snapped his mouth shut. "So violent."

"Are you really surprised?" She took another long pull, held it in her lungs for a few moments, and exhaled slowly. He could actually see the tension dripping out of her.

He shook his head slowly. "No, I'm not surprised. You always did like to strike first and ask questions never."

"That's an oversimplification."

"Is it?"

She considered him and held out the joint. "No. It's really not. The only way to ensure you stay on top is to take out threats, sometimes before they decide to *be* threats."

"You get no judgement from me. You're alive and you're in an enviable position of strength." He accepted it and took a pull of his own. Tristan made a face. He wasn't a smoker; hadn't been since they were kids and he was sure of his immortality in the way only a kid could be. He exhaled on a cough. "Fuck, Te, this shit is strong." He passed it back, a faint buzz working its way over his skin. When was the last time he had pot? He didn't even know. Tristan usually stuck with alcohol, and even then he rarely indulged enough to blunt his edges. Even in Zhao's various properties, it paid to keep an eye out for a knife in the back. That paranoia had saved his life a time or seven.

She kept smoking slowly, the silence settling over them the same way the high did as they passed the joint back and forth until it burned down to the very end. He noticed things in rolling waves. The way the fluffy white robe seemed to dwarf Amarante's lean body, dialing back the years until she could be twenty again. Not innocent. Amarante had never had a chance to *be* innocent. But in those years between that fucking torture camp and Tristan leaving, there was a tiny hope kindling in her that he'd been drawn to.

It was gone now.

She leaned her head back against the chair, exposing the long line of her throat. It drew his gaze to her pointed chin, to the fact that her mouth wasn't painted red for the first time in the last few days. She closed her eyes. "Stop looking at me like that."

"Can't help it."

Amarante lifted her head and shot him a look. "You're not even trying."

"No, I'm really not." He let the buzz smooth out his thoughts. "That guy wasn't just a professional. He was guild."

"I know." She relaxed back into the chair and closed her eyes. "There is more than one guild, though. I can name three off the top of my head, and the only one that advertises their assassins is Manticore."

He snorted. "Yeah, because everyone loves the seven deadly sins. It's one hell of a promotion."

"He wasn't one of them."

No shit. The Virtuous Sins were all women. Tristan was nearly one hundred percent sure that if one of them died, someone else stepped into the role, but for all that their

89

"sins" were advertised, the women themselves weren't exactly running around with neon signs over their heads. He'd met Wrath once, years ago, and he had no desire to repeat the experience. There weren't many things that scared the shit out of him, but that tiny blond did. "That leaves two guilds."

"It doesn't matter." She waved it away without opening her eyes. "The assassin is less important than who hired him. This was a hit."

"Yes." And there was only one person he could think of who would go through such efforts—and pay the hefty fee required to make a guild risk pissing off Nic and the rest of the Warren. Tristan couldn't begin to imagine how high the price must have been. "It was Zhao."

That got her attention. She twisted in the chair, pulling her legs up and wrapping her arms around them. "Did you know there was a second camp?"

He hadn't thought much could shock him. He'd been wrong. Tristan sat up straight. "He closed that camp after you got out."

"Yes, that one. There's another one." She gave a sad little laugh. "It's only a couple hours north of Bueller. All this time, we've been wondering where they set up the new operations, and it was *right there*."

Tristan started to push to his feet and paused. "Te…"

Now she sat up, too. She had to be as buzzed as he was, but her gaze was clear. "You left me. Worse, you left me *for him*. You have to know that I can't forgive that."

"I don't expect you to." He knew how this worked. A future with Amarante was out of the question, even if they could get past all the obstacles in their way. Even if she wanted to. He lifted his hands and let them fall. "Your siblings aren't here to play support. Fuck, no one is here but me. Consider me a stand-in and take what comfort you can."

She lifted a brow. "That is the most pathetic come-on I've ever heard."

He laughed. "That's because it's not a come-on, asshole."

"I stand on my own, Tristan. I have to."

That might be the saddest thing he'd ever heard. "No one stands on their own. Not even me." Surely she leaned on the other Horsemen when she needed them. But even as the thought crossed his mind, he knew it wasn't the truth. Of course she didn't. She hadn't when she was a teenager, when they were living on the street and doing what it took to survive. Of course she wouldn't as an adult when a whole lot more responsibility rested on her shoulders. He pinched the bridge of his nose. "I can't believe they let you get away with that shit."

"It's not hard when it comes down to it. Even when I'm right next to them, I'm apart."

Yeah, she was definitely kind of stoned or she never would have let that truth slip free. "Te." He motioned with his hand. "Come here."

"I don't trust you."

"You don't have to. Just take what I'm offering."

She stared at him for several beats. He had just decided that she would turn away again when she rose to her feet. No shakiness there, but he should have expected as much. He couldn't even tell she was having a physical reaction until she settled in his lap. Little tremors worked their way through her limbs. Adrenaline letdown. Maybe even fear. With Amarante, he could never tell, and he knew better than to ask.

Instead, he carefully wrapped his arms around her and held her close. She felt smaller in his arms than she had been at twenty. Or he was bigger. Tristan wasn't usually the sentimental type, but he couldn't help thinking of the last time he held her like this. He'd just told her that he was leaving, and it was the only time he'd ever seen her break down. The weakness only lasted a few minutes, but as he held her while she cried, he knew it was the end for them and he'd felt like crying, too.

Not now.

Now he simply held her and let himself enjoy the feeling of her body against his. Yeah, it was sexual, but it was more than that. No matter how much she said she didn't trust him, she obviously did on one level or she wouldn't have let him this close.

The thought should have made him happy. He wanted Amarante. He never stopped wanting Amarante.

Instead, he wanted to shake her. His frustration took on verbal form, his normal brakes gone from the weed. He took a deep breath and expelled. "What the fuck were you thinking coming here this unprepared?"

She lurched to her feet. "I'm not unprepared."

"The fuck you aren't." Tristan followed her to her feet, too close. "You're alone, with no support team. Your family didn't even know you were coming."

"No, they didn't." She spun, forcing him to stop or crash into her. Amarante's dark eyes weren't anywhere near the calm she projected when she was outside this room. "And why's that, Tristan? Could it be because they were chasing *you* all over New York City because you were there threatening a fucking college girl. Really classy."

The barb struck true. He wasn't proud of that shit. It was one thing to deal with people in their world who knew the risks when they essentially sold their souls for power. It was entirely another to terrorize a woman by using her little sister's safety against her. And that was exactly what he'd done. "I was never going to hurt that kid."

Amarante's lips quirked the tiniest bit and her eyes went

cold. "Lie to yourself if you must, but don't lie to me. If Zhao gave the order, you would have done it."

He opened his mouth to argue, but finally relented. "Yeah, okay. I would have done it if he gave the order, so I made sure he didn't give the order. I took care of it."

"That doesn't make you one of the good guys, Tristan."

A laugh burst out of him. "No shit, Te. I've never been one of the good guys." He leaned down until his lips nearly brushed the upper curve of her ear. "You're not one of the good guys, either."

"I know." She planted her hands on his chest, but didn't shove him away. Her fingers curled, fisting the fabric and drawing him closer until they were pressed together. "I never got a chance to play on the side of angels. It's the devil for me or nothing at all."

It's you for me or nothing at all.

He had no business reading into her sentence, but that wasn't about to stop him. Tristan meant to have Amarante, to keep her this time. His purpose had begun solidifying from the first moment he saw her in the halls downstairs. He never thought he'd have another chance at Amarante, so he'd settled into a comfortable enough life. Now that she was here, now that she was drawing closer to him as if she couldn't help herself... He'd burn the earth to ash for this woman and he'd do it without regrets. She was his in the same way he was hers.

All that remained was to convince her of it.

"Would you like to see my horns?"

"Shut up, Tristan." She kissed him.

CHAPTER 11

*A*marante didn't know what she was doing. Kissing Tristan was a mistake in a long line of mistakes since she arrived at the Warren. More of them piled into these forty-eight hours than into the last ten years combined. That knowledge should be enough to send her into attack mode, to do something to feel the earth settle beneath her feet. For Amarante, that was always, always fighting.

Except as Tristan's mouth moved against hers, the coldness she carried around in her chest melted and then went molten hot. He obliterated her defenses with a single kiss, spreading fire through her with each stroke of his tongue. With his very presence.

He moved from her mouth to her jaw and down her neck. "Take me to bed, Te."

She shouldn't. Already, her priorities were clouding and shifting because of this man's presence. Letting him closer still…

But that was the problem. Tristan already stood close enough to strike. He had since they were teenagers. He just happened to have physical proximity now instead of simply emotional. The truth was that he'd always been able to hurt her. She handed him the key herself at eighteen.

She stepped back but maintained her grip on his shirt. Without breaking contact, she backed up toward the bedroom. Plenty of time to regret this later. Another person might blame this on the adrenaline letdown, on the pot, on anything but herself. Amarante knew better. She was fully in control, and she wanted Tristan. No matter how foolish it was, she couldn't stop herself.

She didn't want to stop herself.

He kicked the door shut behind them and then they were alone in the room. Tristan moved to close the distance again, but paused. "He's got cameras in every room."

No need to ask who he meant. Amarante released his shirt. "I didn't take you as someone who cared about such things."

"I don't. Except when it comes to you." He gave her a quick grin that did something strange to her stomach. "Give me two minutes."

Amarante wanted to tell him to forget the stupid cameras and keep kissing her before she could talk herself out of doing this. One look at his face told her it was a lost cause. She moved to perch on the edge of the mattress and resigned herself to facing her decision with eyes wide open. It was better this way. Neither of them could pretend like they didn't want this with all the prep work going into it.

Tristan climbed onto the bed and walked to the center, directly under the light fixture. It was more chandelier than just a light, its three descending tiers each containing a delicate pattern of crystals. He took off his shirt and wrapped it around the chandelier. The room instantly dimmed and Amarante stood long enough to flip the light switch, leaving the only illumination from the bedside lamp. He examined his work and stepped off the bed. "That will do."

"Nicholai won't like it."

"Nic will get the fuck over it." He eyed her robe. "In fact, he and I are going to have a talk about boundaries."

She almost laughed. It went without saying that the Warren was riddled with cameras and microphones. They'd already been warned of it, and she'd still let Tristan stick his hand down her pants in that empty boardroom. She appreciated his wanting to keep this private, though.

Tristan moved to stand in front of her and his expression shifted. It took her several long moments to divine it. Desire. He looked at her as if he wanted to devour her whole. She shivered. Something akin to nerves fluttered in her stomach. It had never been like this with Cora. It had never even been like this with Tristan. They'd both changed so much in the last decade. She was already over her head, and she didn't have a plan for what happened next. "Tristan, I—" How to convey her truth without telling him everything? She didn't know.

He was too close, too overwhelming, and too smart. If he realized how special he was to her, even after all this time, he would use it against her. He wouldn't be able to help himself. A scorpion didn't stop being a scorpion just because it liked a frog.

But Amarante was no frog.

She lifted her chin. "Go slow."

Something flickered through his blue eyes, gone too fast for her to identify. "I'll go however you want me to, Te." He lifted his hands and sifted them through her hair. Even though he didn't touch her anywhere else, little zings started beneath her skin. "I like your hair long like this. What made you decide to grow it out?"

"It's mine." Two little words that conveyed so much. When they'd escaped Bueller, she'd cut off all her hair, hacked it as close to her skull as she could. One less thing to worry about taking care of, yes, but it was a purging ceremony for her, a signifier of cutting off the darkness she'd left behind.

Now? Now it was simply hair. She liked it long, liked the ease of keeping it back from her face, liked the silky fall of it around her shoulders. She liked it even more now that Tristan was rhythmically running his fingers through it. Never quite touching skin, but seducing her all the same.

He nodded as if she'd admitted more than she had. Maybe he was right. Tristan had always been adept at reading between her lines. It was one of the things that drew her to him in the first place. It felt like he actually *saw* her in a way that no one else did. Not even her family.

Tristan eased to his knees in front of her. He was so tall, they were almost the same height with her sitting on the bed. This time, when he stroked his fingers through her hair, he kept going, tracing the thick edge of the robe to the middle of her chest. He paused. "I do something you don't like, tell me."

This man...

He had as much blood on his hands as she did. More, even. He gave his allegiance—what passed for it—to an evil man who did evil things. He wasn't a good person.

But as he knelt there in front of her, barely touching her and waiting for her confirmation, he looked at her as if she was something priceless. A gift that would be taken away if he made one wrong move, which made him all the more determined to cherish it. She didn't know how to quantify the look in his eyes, so she forced herself to stop trying.

She wanted this. He wanted to give it to her. That would have to be enough.

Amarante knew better. Of course she did. By the very act of wanting him, she'd crossed more lines than she cared to name. Giving into that desire endangered everything she'd sacrificed so much to accomplish. She couldn't guarantee that she'd be able to think rationally after they crossed this line again... In fact, she could all but guarantee that she wouldn't.

She didn't care.

A nod. She could manage that. "I'll tell you."

Still, Tristan watched her without moving. It was a predator's hunting method, to hold perfectly still and watch its prey so closely, but she didn't feel anything like prey in this moment. No, she felt *seen*. Amarante licked her lips. "What?"

"There's something you're not telling me."

Yes, there was. "There are a significant number of things I'm not telling you."

He chuckled and his fingers flexed against her robe as if he couldn't help himself. He considered her for a long moment. "I can live with that." Tristan leaned forward and she found herself holding her breath. "I'm going to touch you now, Te."

"Do it," she breathed.

He dipped his hands beneath the robe and slowly, oh so slowly, eased it off her shoulders. Amarante unknotted the tie so he could draw the robe down her arms to pool around her hips. Tristan set about reacquainting himself with her body. Or that's how it seemed. He paid equal attention to her arms as he did to her collarbones and finally, her breasts. His longer fingers danced over her skin, pausing at this scar and that. Some of them were old. Those he didn't hesitate over. The new ones gave him pause, though. He touched one on her bicep. "Knife."

"Yes."

Another just above her collarbone. "Bullet."

"Broke the bone, too."

He nodded. "You've been busy, Te."

He hadn't even found the worst one yet. She tried for a smile and failed. "Our life isn't boring."

"That's the fucking truth." Tristan suddenly smiled. "Can't be too pissed about it because you're here now."

But for how long?

It didn't matter. Her future was anything but certain at this point. What did it matter if she took something in these last few days for the simple reason that she wanted to?

She pulled his shirt off and ran her hands over Tristan's bare shoulders. He'd gained new scars in the last decade, too. Some of them had easy sources—blade, bullet, fire—but others stumped her. In the end, it didn't matter. They were symbols of things that had tried to kill him. All had failed.

Touching Tristan felt as close to a spiritual experience as Amarante had ever had. They moved slowly as he divested her of the robe completely and she did the same with his pants. He would never be termed beautiful, but the power coiled in his body drew her. The *man* inside the body drew her. Dangerous, but so much more. Ten years could change a lot, but it didn't change the core of a person. Nothing was capable of such a feat.

He kissed her again, sparking the heat between them to an inferno. Amarante clutched him close, but it was nowhere near enough. "More."

"Anything for you, Te."

Words that should give her pause. They weren't the truth. If he'd truly give her anything, he wouldn't have left.

She pushed the thought away. They had no place in the here and now. She could whip them both with it later if she really needed to. Right now, the next touch, the next sensation, was all she wanted to focus on.

Tristan bracketed her hips with his hands and dragged his whiskers along her shoulder. "I want my mouth on your pussy, Te. I need to taste you, to give us both what we want."

"Do it."

His chuckle vibrated through her, drawing her nipples to hard points and making her thighs clench around his waist. He moved down her body with purpose, barely pausing to press an open-mouth kiss to the sensitive skin below her belly button. Then he guided her legs wide and drew his tongue over her in a long, savoring lick. "Fuck," he murmured against her. "Even better than I remember."

She closed her eyes, but it only slammed her back into the past. To the special place only they knew about, where they'd meet up whenever they had a chance. Tristan felt like the best kind of secret in those days. Something that was hers and hers alone. Until it all blew up in her face.

Amarante opened her eyes. Better to stay anchored in the here and now. She laced her fingers through his hair and lifted her hips. "Again."

He didn't give her grief about her rough commands. He simply did exactly as she told him, dragging his tongue over her again. Perfection. From the tight way he gripped her hips to his whiskers against the sensitive skin at the top of her inner thighs. And his tongue. How had she forgotten this?

I didn't have a choice.

Tristan nipped her thigh. "Stay with me, Te. Don't wander."

The impulse to laugh almost overwhelmed her. Stay with him. That was rich. Amarante managed to muscle it down, though. She lifted her head and gave him as cool a look as she could come up with considering their position. "Perhaps if you stopped dicking around I wouldn't get distracted waiting for you."

His brows lowered even as his lips curved. "Am I being too nice to you?"

Her breath caught in her chest. Now was the time to back down, to reassure him that going slow was exactly what she wanted—what she needed. The latter might even be the truth. It *wasn't* what she wanted, though. She licked her lips. "Yes."

"I'll take that into consideration."

"What—" Her question dissolved into a moan. Tristan flattened his hand over her lower stomach, pinning her to the mattress, and then he stopped teasing her. He sucked her clit hard and then transitioned to the little circles designed to send her over the edge. He didn't hesitate. He simply touched her exactly the way he used to back when he knew her body as well as she knew his. When they learned together exactly what got them off.

Her orgasm burst through her, bowing her back and drawing a cry from her lips. Tristan didn't stop, though. It was like whatever held him back had snapped. He moved away from her clit to fuck her with his tongue, sending pleasure in a rolling wave through her, lifting her higher before she had a chance to truly recover. "Tristan," she gasped. "Too much."

"Do you want me to stop?" He barely lifted his head enough to speak, and he didn't relax his grip in the least.

Did she want him to stop? No, of course not. Yes, definitely. Amarante looked down her body at him, her heart racing in her chest. Tristan appeared... wild. His breath came just as fast as hers, his eyes a little too intense, his hands shaking despite their hold on her body.

This meant something to him, too.

The realization was enough to decide her. "Don't stop."

"I won't stop, Te. Not ever again."

She didn't know how to respond to that. Tristan didn't seem to need a response, though. He dipped his head back down and then there was no time for thinking at all.

CHAPTER 12

*T*ristan couldn't get enough of Amarante. Her strength beneath his hands. Her throaty moans. Her taste on his tongue. He'd spent ten fucking years using the memories of their time together to fantasize about a time he'd be able to touch her again. He hadn't honestly expected to get the opportunity.

If there were people who believed in forgiving and forgetting the wrongs committed against them... Amarante did not number among them.

She dug her fingers into his hair and tugged. "Come here."

He didn't want to move from his current position, not until he'd made her come so many times, she was limp and wrung out with pleasure. But her grip in his hair didn't relent, and so he gave her one last long lick and lifted his head. "I wasn't done."

"Later." She guided him until he was stretched out over her and kissed him. He would never get enough of kissing this woman. The rest of it, yes, but this connection staggered him on a level he still wasn't prepared to deal with. It just reinforced his truth. Amarante and he were connected in a way that couldn't be severed. They would find each other over and over again through the years.

He'd lost too much time with her. He refused to lose more.

She wrapped her legs around his waist and rolled her hips, grinding against his cock. He picked up the motion, enjoying this moment that almost felt like a memory. Back then, they'd fucked around more than once before they finally had sex. This slippery friction, her body moving against his as if they'd been designed for each other, her tongue tangling with his... It was perfect.

But not quite enough.

He flipped onto his back, taking her with him. Amarante let loose a little squawk but regained her balance quickly, straddling him with a glare. As if she wasn't expecting him to pull a move just like that. He ran his hands up her strong legs to her hips and the curve of her waist. He paused on the scar that staggered down one side of her stomach but forced his hand to keep moving. This woman was more than the sum of her scars, and messing with them would ruin the mood.

He palmed her small breasts and then sat up enough to suck first one nipple and then the other. She was just as sensitive there as she used to be, and her hips jerked, grinding down on his cock as he moved back to her left breast. Tristan looked up. "Ride me."

For a second, he thought she might argue, but her dark eyes had gone hazy with pleasure. Finally Amarante shoved him back flat on the bed and looked around. She yanked open the nightstand drawer and pulled out a condom. Her fingers shook, so Tristan extracted it from her grasp and tore it open. He nudged her back a little and rolled it over his cock with a practiced motion.

She raised an eyebrow. "I suppose you've had plenty of practice over the last ten years."

"Something like that." The truth was he'd gone out of his way to purge her from his system. He'd thought if he could just overwrite the memory of her, he might be okay. It took a couple years to realize that would never be the case, and then he'd only taken partners when the loneliness became too much to bear.

The implications of her statement struck. Had she *not* attempted the purge the memory of him? He looked up at her, trying to read her expression. As open as she was right now, she offered him nothing. The thought of her with other people...

Tristan very purposefully set the jealousy threatening aside. Amarante deserved whatever the fuck she wanted. She deserved all the pleasure and happiness in the world. He had hardly been chaste in their time apart, and that was the key here. *Time apart.* It was over now.

He held her gaze, giving her his truth. "None of them were you."

"Don't." She shook her head. "Don't do that. Not now. Now ever."

He opened his mouth and then reconsidered. He had no business promising her shit. Even if he meant every word, they had too much history between them for her to believe it. Only time would do that for him, and it was one thing he didn't have right now. The only option was to relent. "Okay."

Amarante took his cock and squeezed him. There was no hesitation after that. She guided him to her entrance and sank several exhilarating inches down. Her gasp tore at him and healed him, all at the same time. Tristan grabbed her hips. "Slow, Te."

"Yeah." She sounded shaky. "Slow." She braced her hands on his chest and worked herself down him in slow, rolling movements. Inch by inch, until finally, a small eternity later, he was sheathed to the hilt. He tried to keep his grip on her hips light, to let her have full control, to enjoy this moment fully.

She was so fucking perfect. Her strength, her scars, her wicked mind. She took his breath away. Then Amarante began to move. She rode him in languid strokes, and if she was anyone else, he'd accuse her of teasing them both. But this wasn't anyone else. She sought her pleasure in her own time, trusting him to hold out as long as she needed, her touch reaching deep into his soul in a way he wasn't prepared for. He opened his mouth to say… He didn't even fucking know. It didn't matter. This moment was too perfect to mar with words.

"If you could see the way you watch me." She leaned back and braced her hands on his thighs, giving him a completely unimpeded view of her body as she rode him.

He ran his hand down the center of her body and pressed his thumb against her clit, letting her work herself against him. "If you could see the way you look right now."

He wanted nothing more in this moment than for it to last forever. Pleasure sparked down his spine, but he fought it back. He'd last as long as Amarante needed him. In that moment, he'd have done anything for her. "You feel good, Te."

"You feel good, too." Her voice had gone breathy and she closed her eyes, bracing her hands on his chest as she picked up her momentum.

Words bubbled up, words he couldn't allow for fear that it would ruin this fragile thing they built between them in this room. *I missed you. I'm sorry. I love you.* The truth, all of it. He arched off the bed and took her mouth, urging her hips down hard to take him deep. Amarante clung to him and moaned as she came. Tristan held on through sheer stubbornness, stroking her back as she came down.

It took a full minute before she lifted her head. "You know, we're likely to be stuck here all night."

"Yes."

Amarante nipped his bottom lip. "If I promise not to hold you to some ridiculous one orgasm rule, will you promise not to stop until the sun comes up?"

As if she had to ask. He kissed her hard and then toppled her back onto the bed. "I won't stop, Te. I won't stop until you tell me to."

She spread her legs wide, urging him to loop his arms under them and hold her there. "Keep fucking me, Tristan. The only thing I want to feel tonight is you."

He took a few cautious strokes, testing her. She'd said go slow before, but she only moaned and lifted her hips to take him deeper. "You want me to fuck you." His words came out low and dark, a threat and a promise.

"Yes." She grabbed his hips and tried to urge his thrusts.

"You want me deep." He pulled almost all the way out and shoved back in with enough strength to move her several inches up the bed. "Hard."

"Deeper. Harder." She reached over her head to brace her hands on the headboard. A flush spread across her golden skin.

He shifted position, lifting her hips so he held her lower body suspended off the mattress. Then Tristan did exactly what she commanded. He fucked her. Deeper. Harder. Until the wet sounds of flesh meeting flesh filled the room, a perfect counterpoint to his harsh breathing and her moans. Each stroke broke down a tiny piece of the wall between them, and he was determined to annihilate it by morning.

Amarante came with a cry and, this time, he couldn't help but follow her over the edge. He drove into her one last time and ground down, taking everything she offered before slumping to the side. He couldn't stop touching her, though. He didn't want to.

Getting up to dispose of the condom was too much distance, but coming back to the bed to find her stroking herself between her thighs was the kind of reward he could get behind. He stopped next to the bed. "Insatiable."

"Yes."

He crawled onto the bed and knelt between her legs, stroking her thighs as she fingered her pussy. "Fuck, Te."

"That's the idea." She laughed, low and dirty, and then reached with her still-wet fingers to stroke his cock. "Again."

As if he could resist her. As if he wanted to. Tristan reached for another condom. "Again," he agreed.

CHAPTER 13

$\mathcal{A}$marante woke before Tristan, which was just as well. She didn't know how to frame last night. A moment of weakness. That's all it could be, no matter how good it felt to be in his arms again. No matter how safe he made her feel. It was a lie. Tristan might still care for her on one level, but even when they were at their strongest, he chose her father over her. After a single night together? She wasn't fool enough to think she'd tipped the scales in her favor when it came to his loyalty. She doubted he even *had* loyalty.

Nicholai *still* hadn't given the all-clear. The thought gave her pause. Surely the assassin hadn't escaped. The Warren was created specifically to stop something like that from happening. For him to have breached so many defenses and nearly taken out a guest...

Heads would roll.

She just had to make sure hers wasn't one of them. Not yet. Not until she'd finished the task she came here to complete.

Amarante took a quick shower and began her process of getting ready. One layer of armor after another. Hair. Makeup. Lingerie. Clothing. All of it distanced her from the helpless child she'd been all those years ago. All of it sent a message that she was to be fucked with at someone's peril.

"Zhao's an idiot."

She'd heard Tristan rustling around in the bedroom, or she would have jumped when his voice sounded at the doorway. Amarante finished applying her red lipstick and straightened. "You'll have to be more specific."

"He gave you shit about your clothes." Tristan snorted. "As if the suits aren't sexier than most dresses."

"I don't dress for you." She adjusted her top, a structured white and floral piece that went well with her dark green slacks and jacket. It was likely a little too romantic, but if she chose one of her more masculine appearing suits, that would be just as bad. After Zhao commented on her clothing, she was damned if she did, damned if she didn't. No matter what she wore, he would take it as her reacting to his criticism. So, damn it, she'd wear what she wanted.

"No shit you don't dress for me."

What he said finally penetrated and she turned to face him. "You weren't in the room for that part of the conversation."

Tristan didn't even have the grace to look ashamed. "Nic let me have a look at what was going on since Zhao all but banished me."

Another indication of how close Tristan was with the owner of the Warren. Dangerous. So dangerous. If she'd realized how much of a disadvantage she'd be at...

It wouldn't have changed anything. She'd still have come, and she'd still be planning what she was planning. "I see."

"Don't do that."

"Don't do what?"

"Don't start acting like I'm the enemy again."

She gave him the look that deserved. "Tristan, you *are* the enemy. Sex doesn't change that and you know it. How many times have you let sex get in the way of your plans over the years?"

"Zero times." His gaze sharpened. "How many times have you?"

She ignored that. "So you can understand why things can't change." Maybe if she said it enough times, she'd actually believe it. Amarante wasn't one to let emotions get in the way of her endgame, but then she'd never had to dance around her feelings for Tristan, either. Not like this.

"No, Te, I don't fucking understand." He followed her out of the bedroom and into the main area of the suite. Too close. She could all but feel him behind her, and she didn't trust herself to let him touch her again. Already, the temptation to drag him back to bed and spend as much time as they could lost in each other... It was a *serious* temptation.

A knock on the door saved her from having to respond. She took one step, but Tristan moved faster. He held out a hand. "Let me."

"I am more than capable of taking care of myself."

"No one said you weren't."

She considered and discarded the idea of shoving past him just to make a point. It wouldn't do anything but delay opening the door, and she needed space more than she needed to prove she had the largest dick in the room. Instead, she leaned back against the arm of the couch and waited.

Nicholai barely let Tristan get the door open before he charged into the room. "Shut the fucking door."

For once, Tristan obeyed without being a smart ass. He shut the door and leaned against it. It struck Amarante that they were on opposite sides of Nicholai, positioned so he couldn't see both of them without turning, allowing for a surprise attack if one was required. She met Tristan's gaze and saw her realization reflected there. She hadn't meant to do it. She didn't think he had either.

The more things change, the more they stay the same.

Nicholai strode to the wall of faux windows and they flickered, the picture morphing to one of the man who'd tried to shoot her last night. "That is a Typhon assassin."

Tristan swore long and hard, but Amarante couldn't look away from the nondescript man pictured. "Typhon? You're sure?"

"I'm sure." He turned to face them and crossed his arms over his chest. All his suits looked the same, but the creases in this one suggested he hadn't changed from yesterday. The dark smudges under his green eyes backed that assumption up. "He got away."

"The fuck he did." Tristan shoved off the wall. "You have this place locked down more than any other in the world. It shouldn't be possible for him to escape."

"And yet he did." Nicholai bit each word out. "We were less than thirty seconds behind him. He managed to make it to the employee halls and lost us there. Despite having all entrances and exits under watch, he hacked the system and looped the video. We only missed it for about ten minutes, but it was enough for him to leave the property."

A pit opened up in Amarante's stomach. She'd suspected he was an assassin, but she hadn't realized how much she'd relied on Nicholai's reputation to hold up. A double edged sword, that. If he wasn't as good as his reputation, then she might live past killing her father.

She also might be removed before she had a chance to strike.

The clock ticking in the back of her mind picked up

speed. Tick, tick, tick. Not enough time. She never had enough time. She had to strike, and quickly. "No harm done."

"*What?*"

Nicholai didn't look at Tristan, instead pinning her with a cold look. "No, Ms. Death, it is *not* no harm done. He attempted to break the neutral ground and fired a weapon within the Warren. If you were alone, there's a decent chance he would have succeeded. He will be found, and he will be made an example of."

The thought brought her no comfort. No matter if he succeeded or failed, she doubted she'd be alive to see Nicholai enact his punishment. "Typhon is one of the most secretive guilds in existence, to the point where most people don't even know it exists. How could you possibly find this man when you don't even know which of their number he is?"

"That's my concern."

Tristan cleared his throat. "It's more than likely this is all a diversion. The attempt was real enough, but if you're devoted to tipping the scales back into balance, you won't be giving your full attention to this summit."

Nicholai still didn't look at him. "You have my sincere apologies, Ms. Death. I know there is little to make this right, but suffice to say the guilty party will be punished."

He meant that he wouldn't stop with finding the assassin. The reason the Warren was so feared was because it didn't stop with the hand that held the knife. They went all the way up to the person who gave the order in the first place.

She forced herself to stay relaxed. "Good." Had Zhao given the order? It was more than likely. She and the Horsemen had created more than a few enemies over the years, but few of them had the kind of influence to bring in the Typhon guild, let alone pay the hefty tab that had to come from a contract enacted within the Warren. The timing was too much to be coincidence, which meant Zhao was behind it.

The amusement Nicholai tended to display in Tristan's presence was nowhere in evidence as he motioned to the screen and it flickered back to show the early morning mountains. "If you would like to exit the summit, I can arrange it."

"No, thank you," she said.

At the same time, Tristan piped up. "Do that."

Amarante turned to face him. "That's not a decision for you to make."

"You think that assassin was the only one he has up his sleeve? Either the plans changed or he never meant to bring you back into the fold. Doesn't matter what the reason is, because the end result is the same. You're not safe here." He shot a look at Nicholai. "No offense."

"Don't start worrying about sparing my feelings now." His smile was a shadow of what it had been yesterday. He slid his hands into his pockets. "He's right, you know. I can all but assure you that the responsible party won't have a chance to strike again while you're within these walls, but I also doubt they'll try the same way twice. More likely, they'll wait for you to leave and attempt to take you out while you travel."

Tristan cursed. "You have a travel guarantee."

"I also have a fucking peace guarantee in the Warren and look how that turned out." He took a slow breath and when he spoke again, his voice was devoid of all emotion. "We will do our best to protect you and see you safely back to the island."

He wouldn't be saying that if he knew her plans for Zhao.

Amarante didn't bother to try for a smile. Neither man would believe it, and it would only raise suspicions. Perhaps she could use this to her advantage. "Are you taking precautions to ensure that Zhao is protected as well."

Nicholai narrowed his eyes. "You mean are we watching him closely." He hesitated and seemed to realize that he owed her some kind of response. "Yes, we'll be ensuring all his people stay where they're supposed to. This assassin didn't come in with his party, so you'll understand that I have to do my due diligence before I can allow anyone to start lobbing accusations."

"Of course." She pushed off the couch. "Thank you for the update. Is it safe to assume that the meeting today will proceed as planned."

"Yes." His mouth twisted as if he tasted something sour. "If you are in agreement, Zhao is already on his way."

Good. He'd want to see his handiwork, to gloat in his superiority. *Not so superior since the assassin failed.* She glanced at Tristan. Unless that was part of the plan... A fake assassination attempt to drive her and Tristan closer so she'd stop suspecting the scorpion in her bed.

It would be a shitty plan if that were the case. Zhao had to know that Nicholai would take an assassination attempt in the Warren personally, and chase down the responsible party. The risk versus the reward were too unequal. Beyond that, the Typhon guild didn't have a reputation for making fake attempts. It would still be a mark in the failed category, even if that was the end goal. They wouldn't take the job in the first place.

No, if Zhao was responsible—and he had to be—then he'd fully intended to have her murdered last night.

She held perfectly still, waiting for the sting of that knowledge, but it never came. This man wasn't her father. Oh, he'd donated the necessary portion of her DNA to bring her into being, but she'd lived through too much by the time she was eighteen for him to truly hurt her. He could torture her, could kill her, but he couldn't touch her core. He couldn't break her.

Is that what this is about?

But that didn't make any sense, either. There was something else going on, something she couldn't divine out. The only way to do so was to keep moving forward. He wouldn't exhibit surprise when she walked into the room; by this point, he must know that the assassination failed. The ball was in his court. She had to show up in order to find out what he meant to do with it.

Amarante straightened her jacket and slipped on her heels. "Let's go."

"The fuck you're going down there now."

She turned slowly to face Tristan. Even now, with her mind whirling and her plans spinning out around her, she still reacted to him. She still wanted him. Amarante made her gaze keep sliding until she landed on Nicholai. "I assume Tristan is still banned from the meeting room?"

"Yes."

Good. She wouldn't be able to focus solely on Zhao if she had to worry about Tristan, too. She moved to the door and held it open, a clear command even if she didn't give it voice. Tristan stared at her a long moment. "This is a shitty ass idea."

"It's none of your concern."

His jaw tightened and his eyes flared hot. "That's where you're wrong, Te. Your safety is my fucking concern."

"Out." Nicholai didn't touch Tristan, but the snap of command in his voice got the other man moving. They filed through the door and Amarante followed them out. She touched the door knob to ensure it locked behind her, but if Nicholai really wanted to snoop through her things, a locked door was hardly going to keep him out. It was the reason she hadn't brought anything irreplaceable with her on this trip.

That and the fact I don't expect to survive it.

The resolution had settled through her weeks ago. She couldn't afford to doubt herself now. She'd come too far to turn back. The cost of doing so was too high, and Amarante wouldn't be the only one to pay it. She had no choice now.

There was only forward.

CHAPTER 14

"*H*ow the *fuck* did you lose him?"

Nic walked so fast, even with Tristan's longer legs, he still had to work to keep up. His friend veered into a door that led to a pair of elevators. They were nothing like the sleek fancy ones the guests use. No, these were purely utilitarian. He waited until the doors closed to respond. "He had someone on the inside."

That brought Tristan up short. "Impossible." If the consequences for breaking the Warren rules were severe, they were nothing compared to employees who missed the mark. To intentionally do it...

"Nothing is impossible. You should know that by now."

Yeah, he really should. Tristan dragged his hands through his hair and tried to focus. Nari had arrived to escort Amarante to the meeting. She'd be safe enough in the meantime. He still didn't like letting her out of his sight. Zhao wouldn't stop with a single assassination attempt. Not if that was his end goal.

She didn't want his help. She couldn't have been clearer

about that when she turned and walked away without a backward glance. It shouldn't sting, but it fucking did.

He pushed it all away. His personal shit had no bearing on this situation, other than to distract him. Since attending the meeting wasn't an option, he'd do the next best thing and help Nic get to the bottom of this. "Where do we start?"

The elevator coasted to a stop and the doors slid open. Nic held them there with a hand. "I have to ask."

"Then ask."

"You've worked for Zhao for over a decade. You're his right-hand man."

His chest tightened, but he ignored it. "Yeah."

"There isn't a single damn reason for you to put all that at jeopardy for anyone, let alone a woman who doesn't seem to like you very much."

All reasonable assumptions, but Tristan wasn't in the mood to be forgiving. "Ask your fucking question."

"Did Zhao send you to distract her so he could manipulate negotiations?"

Tristan met and held his friend's gaze. "He'd rather chop off my dick than let me anywhere near his daughter, estranged or not."

"That's not an answer."

No, he guessed it wasn't. Somehow, speaking this truth felt like crossing the line more than anything else he'd done to date. When he was with Amarante, it was easy enough to focus entirely on her and forget the rest of the bullshit. Verbalizing it to his friend was different. "I came here for her. Not for Zhao. Not for whatever he's got planned. I'm only here for Amarante."

"Bold words."

"Yeah, well, I'm a bold kind of guy."

Nic frowned. "You're serious." He frowned harder.

"You're going to throw away all that time climbing the ranks for her."

It was more complicated than that, and yet it wasn't at the same time. Tristan hadn't exactly shown up at the Warren with the intention of burning his life down around him, but the moment he realized Amarante still had feelings for him? "Guys like me don't get second chances. Not usually. I have one with her." When Nic still looked unconvinced, he threw him a bone. "A long time ago, I signed on with Zhao and lost her." He hadn't gotten it at the time, not really, but he got it now. "I'm not making the same mistake again."

"No, you're just going to make different ones." Nic pinched the bridge of his nose. "Does Zhao know you're no longer loyal?"

"He suspects." He wouldn't have banished Tristan from the meeting rooms otherwise.

"You all are a pain in my ass. Years, I've run this place without issues. Fucking *years*, Tristan. Now it's all assassins and backstabbing and bullshit."

Tristan snorted and clapped his friend on the back. "Keeping you on your toes."

"I could do without the complications."

Complications like someone trying to kill Amarante. The thought sobered Tristan. "Have I passed your interrogation?"

"Please." Nic shook his head and walked out of the elevator. "We both know you lie as easily as you speak."

That stung, even if he was right. *Especially* because he was right. Tristan wasn't a guy who spent a lot of time preoccupied with honor. The world respected power and power alone. Being honorable was a good way to get killed in his line of work. It gave a person a blind spot that could be exploited. *He* had exploited enemy's blind spots in the past. "I'm not a white hat. I never will be. But if there's one person capable of holding my leash, it's Death."

"That, I believe." Nic led the way down yet another series of halls. This place truly lived up to its name. Back here, without all the glitz that was present in the guest areas, it was easier to remember that they had an entire mountain's worth of rock over their heads. Tristan's skin prickled and he studied the ceiling. It'd held this long. It would hold another lifetime.

They finally ended up in an office that looked like a million other offices out there. Gray walls, gray floor, nondescript deck, computer. Nic pointed at the chair. "Sit."

"When you said you wanted my help, I didn't think you were literally going to put me to work."

"Sit."

Tristan dropped into the chair. Nic leaned around him and tapped a button on the keyboard. The screen cleared and a white woman's face appeared. She was plus-sized and pretty and had deep auburn hair. Tristan would know her anywhere. "That's Gluttony."

"Yes, it is."

He rotated the chair to face Nic. "Why am I looking at a picture of one of the Virtuous Sins? We both know who the assassin is."

"We do…and we don't."

He frowned. "What the fuck is that supposed to mean?"

"I know the assassin belongs to Typhon. He has their style and this whole thing is something they'd pull." Nic hesitated. "But I don't have actual evidence."

Tristan would enjoy this moment of Nic being less than perfect if there wasn't so much hanging in the balance. "You lied." It didn't even surprise him now that he thought about it. The Warren worked because Nic was considered all powerful. Admitting that he had no idea who had come into his territory and attempted to murder one of his guests… It wasn't exactly going to have people giving him a vote of confidence. In their world, reputation was everything.

"I overstated my knowledge." Nic shrugged a shoulder. "Would you like to hear my theory? Or would you rather bitch at me about my underhanded ways?"

"You're such an asshole."

"Pot, meet kettle."

Tristan cursed. "Yes, fine. What's your theory?"

"I think it's the Chimera."

He blinked. That was bad. Really bad. "No one knows what the Chimera looks like. We don't even know gender." He was nearly one hundred percent sure that he'd fought a guy in the hallway, but Tristan knew as well as anyone that that sort of line could be smudged. People saw what they expected to see, and the Chimera was notorious for their disguise skills.

Nic crossed his arms over his chest. "I have a database of every known operating assassin on this computer. It's likely the most extensive in existence right now."

"Cute."

He snorted. "My point is that I while there are some like Gluttony who we know a lot about, there are others that I only have a picture or a small list of suspected jobs."

Tristan made a motion of him to get to the point. "And?"

"I think it's possible that multiple files are the same person—the Chimera."

He turned that over in his head. "That makes sense, but it also doesn't explain what I'm doing here. You have a small army of tech nerds who'd love nothing more than to geek out over this information and run algorithms or whatever the fuck they do to find the answer." Tristan narrowed his eyes. "Are you just trying to distract me so I don't barge in there and fuck up your precious summit?"

"Several birds, one stone." Nic didn't even have the grace

to look sorry about it. "I'm about to devote most of my attention to dealing with the fucking rat in my walls, and I need you to stay out of the way until it's over." He held up a hand, anticipating Tristan's question. "I know who did it. I simply need a few hours to handle it."

And Nic didn't trust his own people to handle this. Knowing the Chimera's working faces would be valuable for a number of reasons. As best Tristan could tell, they were more a ghost than assassins typically were. The face in the hallway had been so nondescript, even though he concentrated, it threatened to slip from his mind. If he knew the other aliases, he'd have a better chance of seeing them coming. That, more than anything else, decided him. "I'll do it."

He nodded. "I'll be back once I'm finished. Resist the urge to wander. I can't be accountable for your safety if you do."

* * *

EVEN AFTER FIFTEEN years of suffering through meetings just like this, Amarante still wasn't used to sitting across a table from someone who wanted her dead. Usually they showed it, something lingering in their eyes or the angle of their heads. Not Zhao. He was just as amused and unflappable as he'd been for the last two days.

Exhaustion rolled over here in a wave. She wanted to go home. The cry of a child in the dark, a part of herself she'd worked hard to eradicate. She couldn't afford to let fear drive her. Not at any point in her life. Fear meant death in too many of the things she'd survived. Fear meant death in this one, too.

She leaned back and cut off whatever Zhao was saying, "I find it strange."

His mouth tightened, but he quickly relaxed into a smile. "What's strange?"

"Your timing. I might believe the rest, but the timing is too suspicious to ignore." She examined her nails, painted a blood red that reminded her of her sister. The thought gave her strength, steadied her. "Are you afraid, Zhao?"

"Excuse me?"

"That's what this is about, isn't it? For weeks we've been closing in. First your Bookkeeper. She was a true delight, by the way. Irrationally confident that you would sweep in to save her, right up until the end." She didn't like thinking about what she'd done to get answers, but Amarante would do it again in a heartbeat. She recited the steps in a cold voice, giving him nothing. "Then there were the other three. Low level partners, I suspect. They all had a vested interest in Bueller, but their loyalty didn't last past the first cut."

There it was again, the slight tightening of his jaw. "I suppose you have a reason for being so crass."

Crass. His audacity left her breathless. "Yes, by all means, we only act out the worst sins humanity can come up with. We certainly don't speak them aloud." She smiled slowly. "That was a good attempt to turn the conversation. Subtle."

Zhao sat back. "You want to do away with niceties. So be it." He spread his hands. "I have an empire filled with dangerous and powerful people who would like nothing more than to annihilate that adorable island of yours. Simply blow it right off the map. The only reason they haven't done so is because of *me*. You are my daughter, and that boy is my son. Come home and let's be done with this."

She considered him as she forced herself to pick apart his words. The threat against the island felt too big, too heavy for her to do more than touch on. If she started worrying about someone bombing it into oblivion, she'd lose what little control she had left. He was counting on that emotional response.

Amarante allowed her smile to widen. "I'm going to kill you."

He jerked the tiniest bit. "Back to being crass, I see."

"Do you know how I got my name, Zhao? You say you sent us to Bueller as a proving ground, but how closely did you watch what happened to us there?" There were so many ways to torture a person. Some left scars on the body. Some caused scars that were more difficult to divine out. When Zhao didn't immediately respond, she kept going. Her tone was perfectly even as if she were discussing the weather. "I was eight first time they put a blade in my hand. At ten, they started calling me Little Death." She'd acted the part of their pet torturer for seven years. Amarante suffered in other ways during that time, but it was the torture that carved out her insides and left her as someone who didn't feel human the majority of the time. "I got very, very good at my craft over the years."

He cleared his throat, the first sign of nervousness. "A proving ground, as I said."

"Mmmm. Yes, you mentioned that. Several times." She folded her hands in her lap. "I chose to hone my skills, to keep them honed, with the sole purpose of punishing those responsible once I learned their identities." She gave him a long look. "To punish you."

"We are sitting in the middle of the Warren." A tiny tremor in his voice, gone as quickly as it arrived.

She'd spent the last forty-eight hours on the ropes, flailing from one reaction to another, dancing to the tune he set. It wasn't until now, until she had icy rage to keep herself at a distance, that she could see his plan all along. If she was spending all her energy reacting, she wasn't thinking clearly. "Did you weigh the odds? Killing me is risky, though I suppose you'll be happy enough if your pet assassin pulls that off. But, barring that, you bring me home as the prodigal daughter returned. Your own little pet monster. And if I don't bow and scrap appropriately, you can always kill me later, when you're away from the Warren's heavy consequences."

"You're speaking nonsense."

"Am I?" She shrugged as if she couldn't care less. In truth, she'd wasted too much time trying to divine out his intentions. She'd forgotten that she didn't give a fuck what he wanted. The only thing she required was his life in payment for the horrors he'd perpetuated.

Truly, it was that simple.

For a moment, she thought he might lose control completely. He was made of stronger stuff than that, though. Zhao drew himself straight in his chair. "If we can't come to an agreement, it will mean war. A costly venture in a number of ways, and a route I think it's safe to say everyone would like to avoid."

Amarante felt her smile go sharp. "That's where you're wrong, *father*. We've already been at war for years. This is simply the cumulation of those skirmishes." She leaned forward. "No matter your numbers and allies, it's not one you can win. Death is coming for you. *I* am coming for you."

CHAPTER 15

By the end of the afternoon, Tristan had a list of ten assassins who could be the same person—Chimera. All were nondescript—medium skin tone, hair that ranged from muddy blonde to muddy brunette, features that were utterly forgettable. When Nic walked back into the room, Tristan all but threw them at him. "You're going to want your computer geeks to verify. I'm sure they can do something with computers to see the bone structure beneath. But, best guess, these are all our assassin."

Nic paged through the list, his eyebrows rising. "More than I expected."

"Makes sense, though. Their whole thing is being multiple people at once, which means they're one hell of a chameleon. With how paranoid most guilds are, it's no wonder they have multiple identities, even within our world."

"Indeed," Nic murmured.

Tristan tried and failed to hold onto his patience. "Now that you're done keeping me occupied all day with busywork, can I leave?"

"Yes." He moved out of the doorway and motioned for Tristan to precede him. "But if she doesn't want to see you, the Warren will respect her wishes."

Something there, something in his friend's tone. He glared. "You're the one who trapped me in her room last night."

"Yes, well, you weren't supposed to be there." Nic didn't blink. "None of that changes the rules, Tristan. Break them again, and I'll be forced to act."

"I'll take that into consideration." He was so close to having the one thing he'd barely dared hope for—Amarante back in his life. He wasn't about to let *anyone* get in his way. Not even friendship would be enough to save Nic if he tried to keep Tristan from her.

His friend's brows rose. "You're feral for her."

"That's one way to put it."

"Does she know?"

"Know what?" He turned to the door.

"That you're totally gone for her?"

Tristan didn't stop. "I've been gone for her from the moment I met her. She knows." Whether or not she realized the implications... Amarante was one of the smartest people he'd ever met. That being said, she had a strange sort of blind spot when it came to people she cared about. Her siblings were one thing. That relationship was established through shared trauma and survival. Even as she held herself apart from them, they *were* a family in every way that counted. She might doubt their use for her once the party responsible for their childhood horrors was removed, but she wouldn't leave them voluntarily unless she absolutely had to.

Unless she was sure her absence would be the very thing that would keep them safe.

Her feelings for Tristan were more complicated. Part of that was his fault. But part of it was just the deep fear

Amarante held that she didn't deserve anything resembling happiness. Not that she'd ever admit such a thing. Tristan saw, though. He always saw her.

Nic followed him out into the hallway and they fell into step together as they headed for the elevator. "She told Zhao that she was going to kill him."

The news brought him a strange mix of pride and fear. "She's more than capable of it."

"I don't doubt that. But if she attempts it while in the Warren, I will skin her alive."

Tristan moved before he realized his intention. He blinked and had Nic against the wall, his forearm against his friend's throat. "You touch her, I'll kill you myself."

Nic didn't move other than to narrow his eyes. "You know how this works, Tristan. There are rules for a reason. She breaks them, then I have no choice."

"Zhao broke them first."

"I have no proof of that without the assassin, and they're in the wind."

He dropped his arm and stepped back. "If you touch her, I'll kill you."

"You'll try." Nic shook his head. "Keep her from going after Zhao and it will be a non-issue."

It seemed simple enough, but Tristan knew beyond a shadow of a doubt that Amarante had only shown up for this summit bullshit to murder her father. She didn't give a fuck about the consequences because she fully expected to suffer them. Anything for her fucking family.

If he was a better person, he wouldn't resent the hell out of her siblings. Where the hell were they while she was here playing the part of sacrificial lamb? Off on their island paradise, playing with their new fuck toys. Amarante had shouldered their burdens countless times over the years, and they were letting her do it again now.

He took another step back. "I'll handle it."

A conflicted expression flickered over Nic's face. "The rules apply to you, too. They have to."

"I'm aware." He turned and stalked for the elevator. The entire ride back to the main floor, he didn't speak, letting his mind chip away at the problem. There was a way through this. He simply had to get enough time and distance to figure it out.

A problem since time and distance were two things he didn't have jack shit of right now.

He stepped off the elevator. "I'm going up to my room, so you don't have to worry your pretty head about my breaking the rules."

"I'm worried about more than that, you asshole." Nic shook his head. "Get some rest. You look like shit."

"Yeah, yeah." It took another ten minutes to make it back to his room. A shower and a change of clothes didn't magically reveal a path forward that wouldn't get the whole lot of them killed.

He wouldn't be able to talk reason into Amarante. She was justified in her need for vengeance. For her to be this close... She wouldn't turn away for god or angels. No, this only ended with Zhao's death, which was the one thing Tristan couldn't allow to happen. The man deserved to die, but the price was too high to do it here. There had to be another way.

He stopped. There *was* a way. A shitty, underhanded way. Something akin to guilt rose at the thought, but Tristan ignored it. He'd never played fair. He wasn't about to start now, not with Amarante's very life on the line.

It took a minute to bottle it all back up, to shove down his stress and anger and fear. To smooth out everything until he looked just as unruffled as ever. His hands didn't shake as he buttoned up his shirt and paused in front of the mirror to ensure everything appeared as it should. It was like looking a week into the past. He'd known he'd see Amarante again; it was inevitable with Zhao targeting the Horsemen. She'd come after them for attempting to take her brother, let alone the other shit they'd pulled. Even knowing that, he'd had an icy wall between him and the world. A necessary thing to ensure his survival.

He turned from the mirror and headed for the door. The hallway was empty, but he expected that. To have his own man stationed outside his door spoke of fear, and Zhao would never make that kind of misstep. Perception was its own kind of battle. Strength beget strength. If he acted paranoid and as if he was afraid, people would assume he *could* be killed and someone would eventually decide to give it a shot.

Tristan knocked, two quick raps. The door opened immediately to reveal Zhao himself. That, more than anything, spoke to how Amarante must have rattled him today. He was instinctively trying to prove dominance. Did he realize it? Tristan was never sure when it came to Zhao.

The man stepped back, allowing him into the room. "You've been busy."

"You instructed me to stay out of the way." He shrugged and carefully turned to face the other man. "I'm keeping myself occupied."

"With my daughter."

Interesting that he had eyes on her room. Either that, or the assassin had already reported in. Though that didn't make sense. Contact while Zhao remained in the Warren was a risk; Nic may be able to track it and use it as proof that Zhao was in violation of the rules. No, this must be something significantly more mundane. He shrugged again. "You knew what she was to me when you recruited me all those years ago."

Zhao's mouth thinned. "I gave you everything, boy. You owe *me* everything."

"Agree to disagree." It felt strange to talk back like this. He usually tried to keep polite and professional and avoid Zhao's legendary ire. Tristan simply didn't give a fuck any more. "You picked me up because you had a use for me, and I've more than provided on that investment for the last ten years. Now, my plans lay elsewhere."

Zhao narrowed his eyes. "I never took you for a romantic, Tristan. It's embarrassing. You can't truly think she wants you. You betrayed her and we both know she's not a woman capable of forgiving and forgetting. She may have a use for you right now, but that ends the moment the summit does. This doesn't finish with the two of you riding off into the sunset together. It ends in blood and death for everyone she's connected to."

There it was. Zhao's true aim. Interesting that he misrepresented it to Tristan initially. All the bluster about Amarante being meant for someone other than him... Apparently, Zhao meant Death himself. The irony might make him laugh if they were talking about anyone else.

He crossed his arms over his chest. "You've done a hell of a job following through on that. Why bother with the summit here if that was always your aim?"

"It's not for you to question me."

It would have been too much to ask for Zhao to monologue a bit at him and give all the pertinent details. Oh well. He'd have to figure it out later. Right now, he had a woman to save from herself. "She's going to kill you."

Zhao sneered. "She wouldn't dare break the hospitality of the Warren."

"Just like you wouldn't?" Tristan raised his brows when the other man's expression went stony. "Yeah, that's what I thought. The difference between you is that she's not afraid to die as long as she takes you out with her. She *will* kill you, Zhao. You've been relying on others to do your dirty work for too long. She's better than you are."

"Your threats are ridiculous."

"Not threats. Predictions. She will kill you before you leave the summit, and she will die for doing it. Those are the facts. I'm not sure how she plans on taking care of you, but Amarante has always been ingenious when it comes to death. It *is* her moniker, after all."

Understanding dawned in Zhao's dark eyes. "You want to save her." He barked out a laugh. "She'll gut you once she learns you were here."

Probably. "I can't win her back if she's dead."

"Tristan." Zhao shook his head. "She's dead either way. You must know that I can't allow her to continue to undermine my operations."

Yeah, he did know that. Which was why he'd find a way to bring Zhao down to remove the threat he posed. But not here. Not like this. "You let me take care of that."

Now interest sharpened the other man's face. "You think you can convince her to alter her path?"

No. He didn't think that for a moment. Tristan could be stubborn as fuck, but he wasn't an idiot. Amarante had been set on this path for revenge—for justice—since she was seven years old and this fucker had dumped her in that place. "Love makes people act against their best interests all the time. No reason that can't apply to this situation." Just not in the way he wanted Zhao to believe.

The man sighed. "You present a compelling argument."

"I do that from time to time."

"You're missing one key element, though."

Damn it, he'd known this was coming. Tristan kept his posture easy and relaxed. "What's that?"

"There's only one way to retire from my operations."

Death.

It always came back to death. In the most literal sense or Death herself. Tristan spread his hands and gave an easy smile. "Simple. You tell everyone you killed me." He knew that wasn't an option even before he said it, but he really enjoyed the way Zhao's eye twitched in response.

"You know it's not as easy as that." Zhao laughed, low and mean. "And you're assuming that I'm more forgiving than my daughter. We both know I'm not."

"Yeah, I guess we do." Now it was Tristan's turn to shrug. "I wouldn't have believed you even if you told me I was free to go."

"That simply proves that you're not as foolish as you're acting right now."

He was already tired of this conversation. Verbally dancing around Zhao irritated him under the best of circumstances, and this hardly qualified. "I wouldn't be the best if I was an idiot."

"And yet only an idiot would come to me with this farce of an offer." Zhao turned away and strode to the clear bottle full of amber liquid sitting on the counter in the kitchen. He never went anywhere without it, a little piece of home.

Tristan watched him pour it. He waited until the other man lifted it to his lips to say, "Hope you had that tested."

Zhao paused. "This came with me from the compound. No one's hands have touched it but mine."

"Sure." Tristan shrugged. "That's what you think." He kept his posture easy and relaxed. "But the other three Horsemen haven't been seen since I was in New York. We assumed they went back to the island, but it's possible they detoured elsewhere. Most of our resources are focused on this location, after all."

He narrowed his eyes. "You're suggesting they could

breach the defenses of the Warren to make an attempt on my life. That's impossible."

"Yeah, it is." He bared his teeth. "As impossible as a Typhon guild assassin making it past the Warren's defenses to try and shoot Amarante in the face."

Zhao very carefully set the glass back onto the counter without drinking it. "Get out."

That was enough confirmation he needed to get moving. Both that Zhao was responsible for the assassin—and that he'd leave the Warren at the first available opportunity. Tristan took a slow step back and walked out of the suite. The door closing behind him felt final, which was fitting in its way. The life he'd spent ten years fortifying and building up was gone. He couldn't go back.

So be it.

He'd never been a man who doubted himself. Doubt meant hesitation, and hesitation meant death. Even when he was a kid, that held true. The death might not be as instantaneous or violent—cold nights killed just as easily as a territory dispute—but the threat of it still hung over his head all the same.

That wouldn't change going forward.

If anything, the stakes had just gotten a whole lot higher.

CHAPTER 16

*a*marante slept poorly.

She wanted to blame it on Zhao and the assassin, but it was more complicated than that. Guilt plagued her, gnawing away at her best intentions. She needed to communicate the location of the new camp to her siblings, but the thought of them walking directly into a trap while she was stuck here, unable to help...

She weighed the lives of the only people she cared about in the world against who knew how many innocents, and she hated herself for it. If she was a better person, she would have made the call as soon as she had the information.

With a curse, she rolled over. It didn't help. Nothing helped, not when every move she made had Tristan's scent rising from the sheets. A reminder of how she'd spent last night, of how perfect it had been. Like before, but somehow better. They had so many unforgivable sins between them. Betrayals of the highest order. There shouldn't be even the smallest possibility of them working.

He hadn't come back.

She flopped over to stare at the ceiling. Surely with everything going on, she wasn't stupid enough to get her feelings hurt because she hadn't seen Tristan since this morning? She knew the score going in. Tristan was the enemy, no matter how gently he touched her or how reverently he spoke in her ear while coaxing her to orgasm. The enemy. *Her* enemy.

At four, she gave up and got out of bed. A single day left to get to Zhao, and she still didn't know how to make it work. Poison was the best option, but he didn't bring any food or drink into the meeting room, and despite the schedule provided at the beginning of this farce, they hadn't spent many meals together. He was being so fucking careful, and it irritated the hell out of her.

She'd made a mistake.

Amarante stalked to the phone in the room and stared at it. For so many years, the brunt of the responsibility fell on her shoulders and she'd embraced that role entirely. If she was taking care of her siblings, at least she knew they were safe. Even as time passed and they stopped needing her. She'd been so sure that this would be her last sacrifice, the thing that would finally ensure their safety.

She'd been wrong.

With a shaking hand, she picked up the phone and dialed. No one should be up at this hour, but she knew better than to assume anything at this point. Sure enough, the line clicked over and Ryu's low voice came through. "I'm very angry with you."

Amarante sat heavily on the chair. "I know." She sighed. "I won't say I'm sorry. I did what I thought was right."

"You made the wrong call, Te. You know it and I know it."

Instinct demanded she argue, but instinct was what got her into this mess to begin with. The one time her instincts had failed her. *Protecting* only worked if she had a plan that worked—and the time to admit she didn't had long since come and gone. "I know."

He released a pent up breath. "Are you okay?"

"No." That drew forth a laugh. "I haven't been okay in a very long time." She hadn't been okay *ever* if she wanted to be perfectly honest. "Do you remember the time after we escaped? When we were in the city and had settled in while you spent all that time learning computer stuff?"

It took him several beats to catch up with the change of subject. "Yeah, of course I remember."

"I don't know if I ever said it, but I'm really proud of how quickly you learned. You're the reason we have the island, and you're the reason it works." Her little brother was a bit of a genius where technology came into play. He'd learned faster than she could have dreamed, had hacked his way to a fortune large enough for the initial purchase of the Island of Ys. All the rebuilding and foundational work they did… All of that was because of Ryu's skills.

"Te, the only reason we survived during those years is because of *you*. You kept us fed and safe. Without you, there is no us, and there sure as hell isn't an island."

"Back then…" Why was the truth so hard? The years should make it easier to slip free, but instead it cemented the words in her throat. She swallowed hard. "It wasn't just me. Tristan was there. He taught me." Without him, she would have turned to murder. It was the only skill she had coming out of Bueller. It might have taken awhile to find a guild, to prove herself, but she could have done it. Death was her trade, after all. Tristan offered her a different path, though she still wasn't sure if it was the right one or not.

More silence. "Tristan… The same man who just threatened Delilah's little sister in order to blackmail her into getting information on us. The same man who just tried to kidnap me a few days ago."

Excuses bubbled up, but she refused to give them voice.

There were no excuses for what Tristan had done or the choices he'd made. He knew that. She knew that. "Yes."

"Fuck."

"That would sum it up, yes." She rolled her neck, but the movement did nothing to dispel her tension. "I'm going to fail. All the things I've put you through, all the sacrifices I've demanded, and I'm not going to be able to hold up my end of the bargain."

"For fuck's sake, Te." A hard edge entered his voice. "I love you, I respect the hell out of what you've done over the years for this family, but don't you think it's time you pulled your head out of your ass?"

Shock made her flinch. "Excuse me?"

"You are not our mother, our guardian, or our god. You're our *sister*. Yes, we've leaned on you in the past, but every single one of us is a fully fledged adult at this point. So put down the cross and join the rest of us in the mortal world."

A slow burn of anger fanned through her, a welcome change after spending three days spinning out. "You put me on that pedestal. All three of you. Don't for a second act like I chose that role. I did what I had to, and when the dust started to settle, we were on different wavelengths. That hasn't changed in fifteen years, and I'm not the only one responsible."

He muttered something too low for her to hear and then raised his voice. "I never said you were the only one to blame for the current dynamic."

"It sure sounds like you are." What was she doing? The others might have petty squabbles between them, but she never indulged in that kind of thing. She couldn't afford to. And yet here she was. Squabbling.

"Come home, Te. I said we'd find a way to get to him and we will. It's not too late to turn back."

Just like that, the wall she'd spent so long perfecting

around herself crumbled a bit more. "I thought it would be easier to get to him. I've failed. I can't do it. The Warren is too well protected." She cleared her throat. "Though that didn't stop Zhao from bringing in one of the Typhon Guild to make an attempt on me."

Ryu whistled. "That's ballsy."

"Yes."

"He's scared of you. He wouldn't have put himself at risk, even by proxy, if he wasn't."

She nodded slowly. "I think so, too. Though it doesn't change the fact that I don't have the ability to get to him here. The Warren will also protect him on the return trip to his compound. Once he's behind those walls, our chances drop exponentially—and they aren't currently high to begin with."

"Come home," Ryu repeated. "We have nothing but time, Te."

Tempting to believe that. She closed her eyes, the truth lingering on the back of her tongue. Once she let it loose, there would be no taking it back. "There's another camp," she whispered.

"*What?*"

"He said they set it up immediately upon Bueller's dissolution. They simply moved operations."

"But we looked as soon as we set up the Island. We've *been* looking."

"I know." Her eyes burned and she squeezed them shut tighter. Of all her failures, this new one stabbed the deepest. "He gave me coordinates. It's several hours north of where Bueller used to be."

Ryu cursed. And then he kept cursing, a long string of vicious words that turned her stomach for what they represented. The Horsemen's failure. How many children had died in the last fifteen years while they were gaining power and influence? How many deaths because they weren't good enough to find this place?

Finally, he went quiet. "Give me the coordinates."

She thought about resisting, but he was right. They needed to know. Amarante rattled them off and waited as the line filled with the click of Ryu's fingers on his computer keyboard. It took him three minutes and then he cursed again. "It's there. It's hidden, but it's there."

She sagged in her chair. "I wanted it to be a lie."

"Me, too." Ryu inhaled audibly. "This changes things."

"It does and it doesn't. Zhao still needs to die." Her stomach felt like it was tied in knots. "But we can't leave them there, even if it's a trap. He wouldn't have passed on this information unless he planned on using it against us."

"Agreed."

The slightest of hesitations. "He's going to make a play for you on the return trip. If not him then another assassin."

"It's probable." She'd never felt so tired in her life and they hadn't even begun to make a difference yet. They would. There was no other option. "If I can get to him—"

"Te, no. We need you."

"No, you don't." The crux of the matter. They might feel like they needed her, but they truly didn't. They hadn't in a long time. It was right and proper. As Ryu had reminded her a little while ago, all her siblings were adults now and more than capable of taking care of themselves and every person who owed allegiance to the Island of Ys. Amarante wasn't some invulnerable deity. She was human and just as fallible as she felt in that moment. "I will finish out the summit. If I can't get to him, I will come home at the end of it. If I can…" She took a careful breath. "I love you, Ryu. Give my love to the others, too."

"Te—"

She hung up.

Amarante stared at her shaking hand for a long moment. For so long, there had been no room for doubt. She had to press forward again and again, often dragging the others behind her. Survival was all that mattered, and doubting herself meant doubting her ability to keep them all alive and safe. So she'd eradicated it.

In this moment, doubt was the *only* thing she felt.

She went through the motions of getting ready, and took the time to slip her pen into the inside pocket of her jacket. Being clothed with her makeup perfectly in place didn't make her feel grounded the way it normally did. She was adrift in so many ways right now.

This is unacceptable. Amarante closed her eyes and concentrated on breathing. A slow inhale. An even slower exhale. Again and again until her body stopped shaking and she was able to pack away her messy emotions, one by one. By the time she opened her eyes, she at least appeared more in control, even if she didn't feel it.

A knock on her door brought her around to face it. Amarante took one step and paused. The last time someone had come unexpectedly, they'd tried to take a shot at her. Nicholai might have a stroke if someone infiltrated his precious walls a second time in as many days. The thought made her lips twist into and almost-smile and she opened the door.

The man himself stood there. Amarante stepped back, holding the door wide, and told herself that she wasn't disappointed not to find Tristan. "What can I do for you, Nicholai?" She even sounded vaguely disinterested, which was a coup all its own considering how she spent the morning.

He took a bare step into the room and turned to face her. "There's been a change of plans."

"Explain."

Gone was the guy with a sly sense of humor who poked at Tristan in her presence. This man was all business. "Zhao Fai has exited the premises. As such, you will be detained here until he reaches his destination to avoid any unpleasantness."

"Unpleasantness." A curious buzzing started in her ears and Amarante moved away from Nicholai. The room wasn't large enough to put the kind of distance she needed, but she made do. "There is still one day left scheduled in this farce of a summit."

"I can't speak to his reasonings. I am simply here to hold up the Warren's end of the bargain. That includes ensuring all parties' safety traveling to and from this location."

Zhao was... gone.

It didn't make any sense. *None* of this made any sense. If he'd wanted to kill her, easy enough to contract that same assassin and send him to the Island of Ys. Their security was impressive, but she couldn't pretend it was significantly better than the Warren's. If he wanted to bring her back into the fold, then why attempt to murder her? For a man who spent so much of life systematically building up an empire in his part of the world, none of Zhao's moves in the last week made sense. Even stretching back further, when he sent Tristan to take Ryu, didn't make sense.

No, something else was going on here, something she was missing.

She turned back to Nicholai. "He broke treaty."

"I have no proof of that."

"I'm aware." She waved that away. "But the fact remains; he broke treaty and I was harmed in the process."

Nicholai raised his dark brows. "You were in a small scuffle where another party took more of the damage."

It stood to reason that he'd be difficult. She bit back a sigh and stared him down. "Is the Warren not concerned with balancing out their scales? I wasn't aware you'd changed the way you operate."

His mouth went tight. "You're not going to let this go."

"Which is precisely why you are going to stop arguing for the sake of arguing and let me have my way."

"You have something you want from me."

She wasn't precisely sure, yet. It was more of a hunch, a feeling permeating her body that nothing was what it seemed. "I would like to review the tapes of where Zhao spent this time when he wasn't in meetings with me."

For a moment, she thought Nicholai would continue to argue, but he finally shrugged. "Give me thirty minutes to get it set up and I'll send Nari for you." His green eyes hardened. "Use that time to pack. You'll be leaving today."

"Understood." If something didn't pop out at her reviewing the tapes, she didn't know what she'd do. Honestly, she wasn't even sure what she'd be looking for. A hunch was little more than an instinct with no factual base, but Amarante learned a long time ago to trust her instincts.

Zhao hadn't come to the Warren for her. She was sure of it.

Now all that was left was to figure out *why* he'd been here in the first place.

CHAPTER 17

*E*ven though he was expecting it, Tristan still breathed a small sigh of relief when Amarante burst into the bar where he sat nursing a single shot of whiskey. She spotted him immediately and veered in his direction, her dark eyes downright murderous. "Did you know?"

"You're going to have to be more specific than that."

She sank into the chair next to him and shot a look around the bar. There was only one other person in the room, an old white man who appeared to be snoring in the corner booth. Amarante still lowered her voice and leaned in. "I will kill you myself if you lie to me."

She wasn't bluffing. Amarante never bluffed about shit like this. "Like I said, you're going to have to be more specific."

"Zhao left."

He turned back to his drink. "I heard."

"You heard." She went perfectly still. "I find it strange that he collected all his people and snuck out in the night, but somehow forgot to take you along with him."

"He and I have decided to part ways."

"You can't honestly expect me to believe that."

He wouldn't in her place. Tristan took the rest of his whiskey as a shot and turned to give her his full attention. "I don't give a fuck what you believe, Te." *Lie.* "It's the truth." *Mostly.* "I am no longer in his employ." *Truth.*

She studied him. "He wasn't here for me."

"Of course he was here for you. Why else would he put together this meeting in the first place if he wasn't here for you? There are a dozen different ways to deal with the threat you pose if he didn't want to talk to you."

Amarante didn't move. No, she played the part of the perfect predator, waiting for him to make the wrong move before she pounced and ripped his throat out. "He shared his meals with a different person every time. Nicholai had them watched, of course, but since they weren't on the official schedule, they didn't receive the level of scrutiny ours did."

"If you really believe that, you don't know Nicholai."

She nodded slowly. "Which is why I convinced him to let me watch the recordings of those meals."

So that's where she'd been for the last few hours. He'd wondered. Nic's policy was to keep warring parties separated, and that included their arrivals and departures. It would be hours yet before Amarante was cleared to leave the Warren. She wasn't the type to hole up in her room for the duration.

Tristan leaned back. On second glance, she was so tense, she was practically vibrating. His skin prickled in warning. "What was the old bastard up to?"

"Carving alliances." Her lips quirked but her eyes remained ice cold. "We've made more than a few enemies over the years. They were all here. The Russian branch of the Romanov family. The Nakamuras. Even the Prietos. I'd be impressed under different circumstances."

Those three families spanned the globe and each brought

the kind of influence that could bring entire countries to their knees. The prickling in Tristan's skin ramped up. "That's impossible." Before coming here, he'd been confident in his place at Zhao's side. The man talked to him, planned with him, brought him into important meetings. If he was staging some kind of global event, Tristan would have known about it.

Wouldn't he?

"It happened." She didn't move.

He scrubbed his hands over his face. She had no reason to lie to him about this, not when it'd be easy enough to fact check it with Nic. It happened. That was a fact. He let his hands drop and pushed the mess of emotions in his chest down deep. Even knowing better, being cut out like this stung. Tristan might have chosen to leave on his own, but Zhao had obviously been planning his exodus even before they came to the Warren. The question of why barely registered. He knew why. She was sitting right here in front of him. "He knew."

"You're going to have to be more specific."

"Zhao." He huffed out a bitter laugh. "He knew I'd take one look at you and burn his shit to the ground in an effort to get you back. He planned on it."

She gave him nothing, still watching him with that eerie stillness. "You honestly expect me to believe that Zhao planned on you choosing me over him, despite all historical evidence supporting the opposite outcome?"

"It's what happened." He sounded defensive and he loathed it. "You're it for me, Te."

"It's infuriating how stupid you all seem to think I am." She spoke coldly, having obviously buried Amarante as deeply as he'd buried his messy feelings. This wasn't the girl he'd fallen for as a teenager. The woman sitting next to him was Death. She tapped her finger on the bar, a slow and steady beat. It took him several long seconds to realize she was mimicking the beat of his heart. She held his gaze. "I'm leaving the Warren shortly. If you try to follow me, I will kill you. There will be no warning shot, no disabling you, no anything. I will kill you, Tristan."

The pieces clicked together in the most obvious pattern. She thought he was a plant. An old trick, that. Let him get close to her in the Warren, and once he was solidly placed, make a big messy breakup with Zhao. She'd take Tristan with her and he'd act as mole and eventual betrayer. That kind of thing would never work on Amarante. She was too smart, too paranoid, too unlikely to let him close enough to harm her and hers—as evidenced by her current threat. He grinned. "You're welcome to try."

Fury lingered in her dark eyes, but she snuffed it out. "This isn't a game."

"You think I don't know that?" He leaned in, getting into her space. "I just found you again. You can shoot me, stab me, fucking try to light me on fire if that tickles your fancy. I don't give a shit. You're mine, Te, and I'm yours. Forever. I let Zhao ruin what we had before. I'm not willing to let him do it again."

"That's not your decision to make. Maybe it was once, but it's not now." She stood, forcing him to move back. "Stay the fuck away from me."

He watched her walk away. The instinct to chase her nearly overwhelmed him, but Amarante didn't make empty threats. She might not be willing to risk herself in the Warren for him the same way she intended to in order to get to Zhao, but she'd still take Tristan out if he chased her down.

At least, she'd try.

Even though he expected it, he still jumped a little when Nic's voice came from behind him. "Trouble in paradise?"

"Fuck off."

Nic sank into the seat Amarante had just occupied. He nodded at the bartender and held up two fingers. "Her escort is taking her in two hours. Do not interfere."

"I have no intention of interfering."

Nic gave him a long look. "No, you have something else in mind."

There were plenty of risks that came from allowing people too close. They became weak spots to be exploited by enemies, or they started expecting a person to change to fit their messy morals and demanding time and energy that Tristan flat out didn't have. Nic wasn't like that. He understood Tristan's role, just like Tristan understood his. They were friends, yes, but the business would always come first. It was a strange sort of relief not to have to play pretend with him. "Zhao used me."

"It appears that way."

Not just once, either. The only reason he'd picked Tristan in the first place was his proximity to Amarante. For ten years, he'd kept him like a loaded gun, ready to point in her direction should it ever become necessary. It didn't matter that Tristan was a fucking asset to the old man. He'd only ever been a tool. In more ways than one.

He cursed. "I feel really fucking stupid right now."

Nic shrugged. "It's a dog eat dog world. Zhao is worse than most. You know that, but it doesn't mean you could have anticipated *this*."

"Don't."

"Don't what?"

"Don't try to make me feel better. You're shit at it." There was no excuse for his oversight. None. He'd had an emotional blind spot when it came to Zhao and he hadn't even realized it until this moment. "That wily bastard played me."

"Yes."

He hadn't felt guilty about how things had played out in the last few days. Tristan was too practical to waste his time on such a useless emotion. Now, though? Now he wanted to deal out violence in a whole new way.

Zhao used Tristan. He'd get over that. As Nic said, he knew what the man was like after working under him for so long. That wasn't what this new surge of fury was about. No, it was because Zhao had used Tristan to hurt *Amarante*. Again.

"I have to talk to her."

He started to push to his feet, but Nic stopped him with a hand on his shoulder. "Rules are rules. You're grounded for the next twelve hours or so. If you try to leave, you will be stopped."

"Are you fucking kidding me?" Even as he asked, he knew the truth. They both had their lines. Tristan's was Amarante. Nic's was the Warren. He let himself be guided back to his seat as the bartender arrived with two whiskeys. Tristan took his and downed it.

Nic made a pained face. "You're such a fucking heathen. No appreciation for the finer things."

"Whiskey is whiskey."

"I'm going to pretend you didn't say that."

He shrugged. "Suit yourself." Tristan rotated to face the bar and blinked. The whole room swam around him, a sickening dizzy swirl. He tried to turn back to Nic, but his body wouldn't obey him. "You basssstard," he slurred.

"You're welcome." Nic caught him as he started to slide out of his chair. "I'm saving you from yourself, you stubborn idiot."

He tried to form a reply, but darkness took him before he had a chance to.

* * *

THE FIRST THING Tristan noticed upon waking was how awful his mouth tasted. He sat up slowly, letting the details of the room wash over him. It was the same suite he'd been in since arriving here. Warm gray walls, tasteful neutral furniture, expensive ass sheets. None of it helped the pounding in his head. "That motherfucker drugged me."

He turned carefully to the nightstand. A glass of water, two white pills, and a note sat there on a fancy silver tray. Tristan picked up the note, taking in Nic's bold handwriting. He really was a fancy asshole.

Death has returned to the Island of Ys. You're free to go.

No apology, but he hadn't really expected one. In the end, Nic was right; if left to his own devices, Tristan would have gone after Amarante immediately. He shook his head, and immediately regretted it when his headache doubled down in pain. Tristan took both pills and swallowed them with the water.

A quick investigation of his suite found his suitcase packed already. Nic being heavy-handed and sending the most unsubtle hint in existence. He snorted and headed for the exit. Under other circumstances, he might stay a few extra days just to aggravate the shit out of his friend, but the stakes were too high and the timeline too compressed to dick around.

Neither Nic nor Amarante had said if they knew what Zhao's plan was. In the end, it didn't matter. After working under him for so long, Tristan had a decent idea of how this would go do. If he'd gotten an agreement for a truce from the three representatives, then they'd hammer out the greater details away from the watchful eye of the Warren. Once everyone was on the same page, they'd bring their combined force against the Island of Ys.

It was the only path forward that made sense. The trick of luring the Horsemen away from the island wouldn't work again. Beyond that, they'd want to send a clear message. Leaving the enemy stronghold intact wouldn't manage that. They had to reduce it to nothing. To burn everything the Horsemen had spent ten years building to ash.

All that would take time to put together, but he couldn't bank on much of it. Zhao would expect Amarante to go on the attack, and he'd take precautions. Would he anticipate her leaving Tristan behind? Hard to say one way or the other. In the end, it didn't matter. Amarante might be the best there was, but she hadn't spent the last ten years learning everything there was to know about Zhao. She needed Tristan, whether she knew it or not.

He simply had to convince her of that fact.

First, though, he had to get to her. Tristan grinned. He always had liked a challenge.

CHAPTER 18

*a*marante stepped off the plane and inhaled the hot humid air. *Home.* She'd never thought she'd see it again when she left a few days ago. To be back again, to have failed so spectacularly… She didn't know what to do. How to feel. Her chest hurt, and as much as she wanted to blame it on her inability to kill Zhao, it wasn't the truth.

No, that fault lay completely with Tristan. Or, more accurately, with herself for letting herself be played a fool by Tristan. Again.

She hitched her bag higher on her shoulder and started walking. Only to stop short when a figure moved out of the shadow of the trees. For one impossible moment, her breath caught and she was certain that Tristan had somehow beat her here. But then he stepped into the light and disappointment flared. Not Tristan. Of course it couldn't possibly be Tristan. No one arrived on the Island of Ys without the Horsemen knowing, and they certainly wouldn't let *him* in.

Luca watched her closely. "Expecting someone else?"

"No, nothing like that." Her voice didn't sound right. She

struggled to adapt the distance she normally wore with ease. "I just wasn't expecting you."

"Uh huh." He still looked like shit. His dark hair was in desperate need of a cut, and he'd lost weight. Normally, he was just as large as Tristan; now he looked downright wan. But considering he'd been shot a few weeks ago and for a few hours, they hadn't been sure if he'd make it, he was doing just fine.

He still shouldn't be out and about by himself. "You should be resting."

His dark eyes flared. "You're lucky I don't hogtie you and haul you back to Pleasure on the back of a cart. What the *fuck* were you thinking, Te?"

She stopped short. "You know exactly what I was thinking."

"Yeah. I do." He stalked closer. "We don't need you to protect us anymore. We haven't for years. We just need *you*." He stopped and cast a critical look over her. "You look like shit."

"Funny. I was thinking the same thing about you."

The anger didn't quite die in his eyes, but it dimmed. "We'll get the bastard."

They kept saying that. Over and over and over again, until it was more mantra than reality. She'd had her chance to get Zhao, had sat less than three feet from him. Instead of killing him like she planned, she'd fucked her old flame and allowed Zhao to dance circles around her while she was distracted. "I fucked up."

Luca lifted his arms, just a little, the tiniest of invitations. Amarante didn't think. She stepped into him and hugged him tightly. His shock only lasted half a breath and then he carefully wrapped his arms around her. Neither of them were big touchers. They'd had that part of them driven out when they were far too young. Another loss to lay at Zhao's feet.

But sometimes a hug really was needed.

She inhaled the familiar scent of her brother and some of the tension filtered out of her. "I'm sorry."

"Me, too."

Her throat prickled and she stepped back. Luca immediately dropped his arms and released her. She looked away. "The others are back in the hub?"

"Yeah." He gave a rueful grin. "You're going to get your ass handed to you. Everyone was scared, and you know how we react to that."

With anger and violence. Never the latter against each other outside a sparring ring, but there were plenty of harsh words exchanged over the years. Considering how badly she'd scared them all, she was in for it. "We don't have time for that."

"We're family, Te. Make time."

She fell into step next to him as they followed a little footpath to where he'd parked the golf cart. There were no cars on the island. It was too small and, while there were a scattering of private villas on the western coast, the only place they truly changed was the eastern coast that wrapped around the natural bay. Two casinos and a boardwalk full of ridiculousness between them. The northern casino, Pleasure, was their base of operations and their current destination.

Luca parked the cart around the back of Pleasure, near the dock they kept for Horsemen use, and grabbed her bag. She tried to take it, but he glared. "Now is not the time to argue."

"I'm being practical. You're still hurt."

"Shut up, Te." He hauled the suitcase up to the door, leaving her to follow.

She hesitated. Amarante had faced down her siblings more than once over the years. Family, no matter how close, fought from time to time. They were no different in that respect. But this was different. She'd lied to them when she gave them the timeline for the summit. And then she'd waited for them to be distracted rescuing Ryu's woman's sister in New York and snuck out like a thief in the night. All with the intention to die for them.

To die for vengeance.

"Te."

She looked up at Luca. "It wasn't supposed to be like this."

A remembered pain flashed across his face. "I know. A lot of things weren't supposed to be like this." He dredged up a smile. "But we're doing okay considering."

Okay wasn't good enough, even if it was the best they could manage. The sword hanging over their head was supposed to be gone now, but instead it was only stronger. "I'll get us through this."

Luca shook his head. "*We'll* get us through this." He pushed open the door. "Come on. The longer you keep them waiting, the more time they have to think up all the things they want to yell at you."

Guilt flared, hot and uncomfortable. Amarante didn't normally waste time with such a useless emotion, but she'd never stepped in it quite so thoroughly as she had the last week. Knowing that she wasn't supposed to survive to deal with the emotional fallout—that she'd felt relief at that when she left—only made the guilt worse.

They wove their way through the passageways that weren't available to the public. The two casinos on the island were set up similar to the Warren in that way, though the Warren's passageways seemed significantly more complex.

All too soon, they stepped into the hub. It was a large room with one side devoted entirely to monitors and several computers, all of which Ryu used to keep track of the comings and goings of people of interest. The rest was divided into a kitchen with a dining table and a full range, and a living room with overstuffed couches. Several hallways led off the other side of the room, each going to one of the Horsemen's private suites. Not just the Horsemen now, though. Luca, Kenzie, and Ryu had all found partners in the midst of the chaos of the last few months. She was happy for them. Truly, she was.

But she couldn't look at them scattered around the room without thinking about the man she'd left behind at the Warren.

Tristan wouldn't fit in here. He enjoyed fucking with people too much. It was part of the reason she'd kept him away when they were teenagers. That, and she'd wanted something entirely for herself. She didn't know if she regretted that now. Either way, it was too late to worry about it.

Luca dropped her suitcase in front of her hallway and walked to where Cami, the former Princess of Thalania, sat. She touched his arm and let him tuck her against his side, but the look she sent Amarante was downright icy.

I deserve that.

Kenzie sat on the table, her legs swinging easily. Anyone who wasn't familiar with her would think she was just nervous, but Amarante knew better. The swinging would give her momentum if she chose to jump off the table and attack. The man in the chair next to her put a big hand on her thigh, stilling her. Liam, former right hand man to one of the most powerful crime families in Boston.

And finally, inevitably, there was her brother by blood, Ryu. As usual, he sat in the rolling chair in front of his computers, his expression unreadable. The only difference was the woman in his lap. Delilah, an exotic dancer who worked in Pleasure. She appeared relaxed, but the careful way she was draped over Ryu spoke of using her body to remind him to stay in place. To not rush into anything.

Their partners made them better. Stronger. More complete. They tempered her siblings' rough edges. The knowledge was bittersweet, to say the least. They truly didn't need her any longer.

Kenzie started to hop off the table, but Liam wrapped an arm around her waist and scooted his chair back to pull her into his lap. She huffed out a breath. "I was just going to greet my dear sister."

"With a fist to her face?"

The smile she gave was sharp enough to cut. "Just a punch or two."

Amarante gave a sharp smile of her own. "Try it." This, she knew how to do. Fight. Argue. Poke and prod and manipulate until the people around her gave her the desired outcome. Easier to fight than to deal with the complicated emotions curdling her stomach.

Ryu carefully set Delilah on her feet and moved forward. "You failed."

The sick feeling in her stomach rose into her throat. "Yes. I failed."

"Thank fucking god." He jerked her into a crushing hug. It drove the breath from her lungs and it didn't matter because she was hugging him back and, oh god, what was going on with her eyes. Ryu squeezed her tighter. "Never, *ever* do that shit again, do you hear me? He's taken too much. He doesn't get to take you, too."

Other, smaller arms came around her from the back and then Kenzie was there, holding her between them. "You fucking asshole, I was so worried about you."

Luca ruffled her hair and she lifted her head to shoot him a look, even if she didn't have the heart to put any oomph behind it. Right in that moment, surrounded by her family, she finally had to admit that her mistakes weren't only that she didn't manage to kill Zhao. It was that she'd gone after him alone in the first place. "I wanted to keep you safe."

"You think losing you won't hurt worse than anything that's been done to us so far?" Kenzie pulled back and smacked her shoulder. "Don't be stupid. You know better."

She moved back and then there was only Ryu. Amarante looked up at her brother's face and pressed her lips together. "I'm sorry."

"I know." He gave her one last squeeze and released her. Just like that, the soft moment passed and they were all serious again. "Let's talk about next steps."

Amarante took the single chair and the rest of them piled onto the remaining furniture. It felt strange to look at six faces instead of three. Strange, but right. She took a breath. They wouldn't have peace until this was finished, and if they didn't finish it fast, they might lose. She hadn't anticipated Zhao reaching out to other enemies, and that was her mistake. She should have known he'd do anything to remove the Horsemen from existence. They were a living representation of his failure with Bueller.

And she still didn't know *why*.

She took a careful breath. "He played me. For three days, he gave me the runaround with a bullshit story about Bueller being a proving ground for me to take the role as his heir."

Kenzie snorted. "He had to know you're too smart to fall for that shit."

"It didn't matter if I fell for it or not. He wasn't there for me." She pressed her hands flat to her thighs. "While I was occupied and distracted, he set up meetings with the Romanovs, the Nakamuras, and the Prietos."

Cami cleared her throat. "But Dmitri and Keira Romanov were here during the Wild Hunt. They seemed to be… Well, not totally evil."

"They're the New York Romanovs." Ryu rubbed his hands

over his face. "They're part of the overall Romanov family, but they mostly operate separately since Dmitri took over. The Russian branch of that family is more extensive and significantly more dangerous. Which is saying something." He lifted his head. "That's why he gave you the correct coordinates for the new camp. Even if he didn't manage to kill you, that's guaranteed to distract you while he gets his play lined up. We attack the camp, we leave the island undefended."

"The camp itself could be the trap, too." Luca's gaze was on something long since buried in the past. "He'll have planned for all options."

That's what she thought, too. There was still the assassin to contend with as well. It was probable that, since she was still alive, the contract remained open. The others had to know. She took a deep breath. "There's more." Amarante quickly filled them in on the assassin and the rest of what happened, carefully leaving out mention of Tristan. Kenzie shot her a sharp look as she finished up, but luckily her sister didn't feel the need to put her on the spot. She'd pay for that later, no doubt.

Luca sat back. "We can't keep him out."

"I know." If the Warren couldn't, they stood no chance. They *might* see him coming, but she had her doubts about that as well.

Kenzie gave a wicked grin. "I have an idea."

Liam sighed. "If it's got that look on your face, it's either brilliant or scary as fuck."

"Why limit me? I think it's both." She turned that look on Amarante. "I think you should call in Lust. Or maybe not her, since her skillset won't match this. Maybe Wrath or Greed would be better fits. If you're right and this guy is Chimera from the Typhon Guild, then he's the very definition of a high stakes target."

Liam cursed. "I was right. Brilliant and scary as fuck."

Cami was looking at Kenzie as if she was crazy. "You're going to start a guild war."

"On the contrary. It's not personal if we're paying. It's just good business."

Ryu started rubbing his temples the way he did when that impressive brain of his was thinking hard. "It might be the best option. Typhon's reputation is too important for them to call off a hit, even if we're willing to pay through the nose for it. If anyone can find this guy and take him out, it's one of the Virtuous Sins."

She took a careful breath. Her friendship with Lust might not survive taking on this contract. How could it when things would be forever changed between them?

So be it.

"I'll call Lust."

CHAPTER 19

*J*t took several hours before Amarante managed to make it to her room. She dropped into the chair next to her desk and stared at the phone. She and Lust were friends after a fashion, but they hadn't spoken since the Wild Hunt a few months ago. That length of time without communication wasn't rare, but this year one of the Virtuous Sins had competed—and lost—in the Wild Hunt. Tempers were bound to be sore, and she hadn't bothered to check in with Lust after the fact. She should have.

Amarante took a deep breath and dialed before she could stall longer. The line rang and rang. It wouldn't surprise her if Lust didn't answer. She tended to disappear while she was on jobs, and that meant leaving her personal phone behind. Each Sin had their specialty, but Lust was one of the only ones who inserted herself into her mark's life in order to get close enough to kill. It was entirely possible she was on one of those jobs right now.

Equally possible that she was pissed at Amarante.

Finally the line clicked over and her warm voice came through. "I'm surprised to be hearing from you, Amarante."

161

So, it would be like that, then. She breathed out a sigh that wasn't quite relief. "Cora." The slightest of hesitations. "Lust."

The warmth didn't quite leave the other woman's voice, but when she spoke again, she was crisper. "Not a social call, then?"

"Unfortunately, no." Worse, after spending the night with Tristan, she didn't know if she could go back to her rare times with Cora. She cared for the woman. The sex wouldn't work if she didn't. But she didn't love her with the same insane desperation that she felt for Tristan.

Love.

The very idea should be laughable. Tristan was the enemy, the betrayer, the one who would always turn his back on her. She was a fool to care for him at all, let alone *love* him. But Amarante tried very hard not to make a habit out of lying to herself. To others, maybe, but never to herself.

She loved Tristan. She'd never stopped loving him, even when he tore her heart out of her chest and took it with him. Even knowing he was almost certainly still working for Zhao and not to be trusted. Apparently she was a fool, after all.

"Pity." Now it was Cora's turn to hesitate. To sigh. "Do you want to talk about what happened with him?"

She almost said no, but in the end, who would understand quite like Cora? "How did you know?"

Cora laughed. "That's a silly question, and you know it. Criminals gossip more than anyone else. Even though you were discreet, one of Sloth's little birdies heard a rumor that Death had her head turned by a certain blond. He's the one, isn't he?"

No use denying it. Cora was the only one who knew the full story of Tristan. "Yes."

"Hell."

"That sums it up nicely." She gave herself a shake. "In the

end, it's immaterial. I left him at the Warren, and I have bigger problems than my heart."

"I'm sure you siblings have already ripped you a new one for doing something so foolish as to face down Zhao alone, especially since I'd bet good money that you went there intent on killing him."

She cleared her throat. "That's immaterial, too."

"Amarante." Even though she couldn't see her, she knew without a shadow of a doubt that Cora had a resigned look on her gorgeous face. "You know I'm here for you."

"I know."

"Okay." She blew out a breath. "Okay. If you're not calling to catch up, then this is business?"

Once she went down this path, there was no going back. Her friendship with Cora would be forever altered by this messy business. As much as she hated the thought of that, ultimately there wasn't a choice. Her family mattered more than anything, and this would keep them safe.

She closed her eyes. "Yes." There it was. No going back now. "How much do you know about what went down in the Warren?"

"Lots of meetings with you and Zhao. He bolted early without warning. You and Tristan spent a significant amount of time holed up together. And the whole Warren went into lockdown for about twelve hours. Even Sloth couldn't get into their system during that time."

Did Nicholai know that the Virtuous Sins had eyes inside his system? If they did, it was more than likely others did as well. Maybe that was how Chimera got in, rather than a traitor. She'd decide later whether or not to pass that information on to him. "A man tried to shoot me in the face. The Warren is nearly one hundred percent sure that they've positively identified him as the Chimera, operating out of the Typhon Guild."

163

Cora whistled. "They brought out the big guns for you."

"Yes." She tapped a single finger on her desk. "He'll keep coming for me until he's completed his assignment, and if he can get into the Warren, he can infiltrate the island."

"Definitely. Getting into the casinos might be a little harder, but I don't expect you're going to do something smart like bunker down and wait this out."

"We're going after Zhao." She couldn't tell Cora the rest—Zhao's plans and his familial relation to her. As much as she trusted the woman, in the end Cora answered to her handler and her sisters. If a hit ever came in on Amarante or one of the other Horsemen, she wouldn't have a choice if their company took the contract.

Cora sighed. "That's what I thought."

"I need him dead, Cora. I don't care what it costs."

Silence stretched out between them and Amarante found herself holding her breath. Cora might say no. It was within her prerogative. It might even be preferable. Yes, it would complicate Amarante's life, but in the end she was confident in her abilities. If not for the compressed timeline, she'd have handled this herself. As it was, she couldn't afford to be distracted.

Finally, Cora said, "This isn't a job for my skillset. I'll have to take it up the line."

"I suspect it will fit with either Greed or Wrath." Greed specifically took out targets that were considered impossible by anyone else. The more challenging the target, the better. And Wrath? Wrath made examples of people. Amarante had never met her, but she had a terrifying reputation. At least, terrifying for those who ended up on her list.

"Yes." The warmth filtered out of Cora's voice, leaving her coolly professional. "I'll have an answer within the hour."

"Thank you."

"Don't thank me yet. You haven't seen the bill." She hesitated. "You were right to call me, Amarante. Even if this changes things. It was the right call."

"I know."

"Keep your phone close." Cora hung up.

Amarante set the phone down and released a long breath. For better or worse, it was done. She pushed to her feet, feeling a hundred years old. There would be no rest once things got rolling, but she needed to take what sleep she could tonight. At the top of her current priority list was a shower, though.

She walked down the short hallway to her bedroom, each foot taking more effort than it should to cross. An hour. She'd have an answer from Cora in an hour, and then she could sleep. It wouldn't be enough to save her from nightmares—not tonight—but it was better than nothing.

She was so tired, it took two full steps into the room before she realized she wasn't alone. Amarante blinked at the figure lounging against her bed. "What the hell?" She dove for her dresser and the gun she kept there...only to come up empty.

"I know you're pissed, but shooting me seems a little extreme, even for you."

That voice. She knew that voice. She stalked to the light switch and flicked it on. Sure enough, Tristan sat on the edge of her bed, her guns dismantled on the comforter next to him. He'd found all six of them, which meant he'd been here for a while. "Give me one good reason I shouldn't kill you right now."

"You love me."

Her heart beat unnaturally loud in her ears. "I said give me a good reason."

His smile didn't falter. "I love you, too, you know."

He did *not* just say that. "You're not capable of love."

"Apparently I am." He shrugged as if he hadn't just

165

dropped a bomb on her. "I know I fucked up—more than once—and I know that apologizing won't do shit to make things right. I am sorry, by the way." He spread his hands. "So I'm going with the next best thing."

Surely her head wasn't actually spinning on her shoulders, no matter what it felt like. "The next best thing," she repeated.

"Yes." He gave her a wicked grin. "I'm going to give you Zhao's head on a platter."

This was a trap. It had to be a trap. There was absolutely no way that Tristan had spent exactly three days with her and suddenly developed the kind of love that would make him turn his back on Zhao. If he was even capable of that emotion—and the jury remained out on that—he would have felt it when they were younger. He would have chosen *her*, not money and power. He didn't then, and he certainly wasn't doing it now. "Get out."

"Unfortunately, that wasn't one of the options." His smile fell away, his gray eyes going serious. "I know you won't thank me for saying it, but you need me, Te. His compound is just as much a fortress as the Warren is. More so in some cases. You'll never dig him out of it without help. *I* am that help."

She can't trust him. She would be worse than a fool to trust him. He betrayed her time and time again, and now he somehow managed to sneak into one of the few places she felt safe. "How are you here?"

"Not with the help of friends." Tristan made a face. "I didn't take Nic for someone who had a stash of roofies on hand, but here we are."

"That's not an answer." Not only is he on the Island of Ys, but he's *here* in the very center of their home. It shouldn't be possible.

Tristan stood slowly, his expression serious. "I plotted my

way in here months ago. Before you ask, it's not information I shared with Zhao. But I figured I'd have to get to one of you eventually, and I like to be prepared."

"Get to one of us." She seemed incapable of doing more than repeating what he'd said. "You figured out a way into the hub to kill one of us."

"Whoa, hold on there." He held up his hands. "Maybe some light kidnapping. I wouldn't kill one of your siblings, no matter how big a pain in the ass they are. I sure as shit wouldn't kill *you*."

"Some light kidnapping." Damn it, she was doing it again. She took a step back and reached out for the knife she kept in a sheath behind the dresser. He'd missed that one. "Get out."

He didn't move, didn't even look at the blade in her hand. "You need me, Te. You can like it or not, but you need me. I fucked around long enough. I'm not going to let that bastard murder you when I just found you again."

"*Found me.*" She practically spit the words. "You always knew where I was. It's never been a secret."

Another of those shrugs that meant absolutely nothing. "Yeah, I did. But I assumed that if I showed up, you'd cut my throat."

"A correct assumption."

He lifted his hands and dropped them. "I didn't think there was anything left to chase down, so I moved on with my life as best I could." He glanced away. "I didn't know he was behind Bueller until recently."

"And yet you still stayed."

"No shit, I still stayed. He was gunning for *you*. You think my leaving would be an asset? I'd be flying as blind as you are now. No matter if he changes his codes, I've spent a fucking decade ensuring he wouldn't be able to cut me out whenever he felt like it. That time and effort can work in your benefit, but you have to let me help."

"I don't *have* to do anything."

He cursed. "If you don't, they'll die. You'll all die. You don't stand a chance without me."

That's what she was afraid of. If there was a way to get to Zhao in his compound, they would have found it by now. She would have struck weeks ago instead of going through the farce at the Warren in an attempt to murder him, even at the expense of Amarante's life. Now, with him working with the other families they'd managed to make enemies of over the years, the timeline had compressed. They'd only get one chance at this. "There's no way I can trust you."

"There's no way you can afford not to."

CHAPTER 20

*T*ristan found himself holding his breath as Amarante studied him. He'd laid out his argument in a way she couldn't ignore. Whether she actually went on to ignore it was up in the air. The woman could be logical and icy calm, but she hadn't displayed it as much since meeting her father. Zhao would be counting on his presence —his history—to throw her off her stride enough that he'd have the advantage. Tristan couldn't let it happen. One missed step and he'd lose Amarante for good.

He didn't even truly have her yet, and he'd lose her.

Finally, she crossed her arms over her chest. "My brothers will most likely try to kill you."

He shrugged. "I expect no less." He didn't have many people he cared about in this world—he sure as hell didn't have an actual family—but he could imagine he'd react the same way in their shoes. Though Tristan wouldn't *try* to kill anything. He'd simply take care of the threat.

Amarante sighed. "My sister might actually kill you."

This time he couldn't quite pretend indifference. Kenzie —War—was a key component in boosting the Island of Ys to its current place of notoriety. She was loud and brash and had played the White Stag in every Wild Hunt they'd conducted except one, acting as bait to the hunters who came to the island in search of whatever prize that year offered. Beyond that, she was the ringleader of the main events they offered the rest of the time. Fights and fucking and all sorts of revelry. One crossed War at their peril, and even Tristan was wary of the woman. "She's got quite the reputation."

She raised an eyebrow. "If we survive this, I'll let you have a go at her in the ring. I won't want to hear any bitching when she knocks you out in the first round, though."

"Nah, I'd rather go into the ring with *you*."

That got a reaction, a tiny twitch of her lips. "I don't fight in the ring."

Understanding rolled through him. "You can't pull your punches."

"Something like that."

Tristan grinned because he knew it would aggravate her. "You managed to do it with me."

"That's not what happened."

He took a slow step toward her. "Yes, it is. You forget, Te. I know you. I'm good, but I'd wager that you're better. If you wanted to rip out my throat any of those times we went round in the Warren, you would have done it."

She didn't retreat, just watched his progress with narrowed eyes. "And bring down Nicholai's wrath? Don't be stupid."

"I attacked you first both times. You had justification and the videos would prove it." He stopped a bare inch from her. "You chose not to."

"Maybe I forgot."

He snorted. "Give me a little credit, Te. That mind of yours is constantly examining paths forward and picking the best one to suit your option."

"Not always." She spoke so softly, he barely heard her despite being so close. "You touch me and I stop thinking. It makes me crazy."

Something unfurled in his chest, though he couldn't begin to say if it was relief or guilt. He'd thrown out the assumption that she loved him, but he hadn't really known. Even when she fired back her response, he hadn't *known*. "You do love me."

"Yes." She slowly, haltingly, lifted her hands to place them on his chest. "It's still not a good enough reason not to kill you, let alone to trust you."

He covered her hands with his own. "Don't trust me, then. Use me. I'm a fucking valuable asset and I might just keep you and the people you care about alive. That's worth a whole hell of a lot; don't act like it's not."

"Tristan..." Her mask cracked and for a moment, she looked so agonized, he wanted nothing more than to yank her into his arms and hold her until the moment passed. It wouldn't help, though. Not when *he* was the reason she had that look on her face to begin with. Amarante's breath shuddered out. "I promised myself I wouldn't ask."

"Ask." He pressed his hands more firmly against hers, anchoring her to him. "I'll answer truthfully."

For a moment, he thought she'd retreat. He couldn't hold her if she wanted to go. He knew better than to try. The only option was to wait her out and see which side of the line she'd land on. Finally, Amarante looked up at him. "Why did you leave? Why did you choose him over me?"

It was like stepping back into the past. She'd stood just as close and all but begged him to stay in that shitty room that might have been falling down around them, but was *theirs* in a way nothing else in the world was. Tristan had walked away then. He wouldn't make the same mistake ever again.

He cleared his throat. "I didn't have shit to offer you."

"I didn't ask—"

"Let me finish, Te. You wanted the truth. I'll give it to you. You just have to let me finish." He waited for her nod of confirmation to continue. "Yeah, I taught you to steal, how to avoid the cops, and how to keep your family alive. But that's all I knew. I didn't have resources. I was barely getting by, and with your brother learning his computer shit, *you* were going to leave *me* soon."

Her brows drew together. "I wouldn't have left you."

"No, you wouldn't. You would have brought me with you and I would have lived under you the same way your siblings do. We wouldn't have been on equal ground. No matter what you said, you'd start holding yourself back from me the same way you do from them."

Now she was full on glaring at him. "That's bullshit."

"Maybe." Tristan shrugged. "Hindsight is a bitch, and I don't have a convenient time travel machine to test out your theory. But the fact remains, that's what I was feeling back then. What do you want me to say, Te? I was twenty-three and scared shitless that I was going to lose you. I knew it would piss you off if I signed on with Zhao, but he offered me more money than I could have dreamed of and a promise for training to earn more. I always planned to come back for you once I had my shit set up." He made a face, the pain of that day still lingering despite his best efforts. "But when I came back, you were already gone."

"Of course I was already gone. The second you left, it was too painful to stay there. Every time I turned around, I caught myself looking for you. It was easier to simply leave." Now it was her turn to shrug. "Ryu cracked his first account the week after you left, so we had money for the first time. We relocated to California for a few years while we built up the capital to make the island purchase happen."

"And the rest is history."

"And the rest is history," she repeated. Amarante didn't drop her gaze. "It wouldn't have mattered, you know. Even if you found me when you came back. It hurt too much for me to stand looking at you."

He released a pent up breath. "I've said it before, and I'll say it again. I don't expect your forgiveness. I don't need it, Te. I just need you."

"You can't say things like that."

"I just did."

She clenched her fists around the fabric of his shirt. "It will never work."

"Won't know until we try."

"My family hates you."

"Your family has met me under less than ideal circumstances. I'll grow on them. They won't be able to help themselves."

She didn't smile. "Zhao and the others will likely attempt to kill us all."

"Attempt being the key word there." He let his smile drop. "We can keep doing this back and forth, but you already made your choice, Te. Are you trying to convince me or yourself?"

Her shoulders dropped the tiniest bit. "I'm... scared."

He would fight literal dragons for her, but that wasn't what she was saying. She wasn't scared of some outside force. She wasn't even scared of Zhao. No, she was scared of the hurt *he* could bring her. "I can't promise never to make mistakes. Hell, I can practically promise that I *will* make mistakes. The only thing I can promise is that you will be my priority, Te. Just you."

"This is a mistake."

"Only one way to find out."

She worried her bottom lip. "Okay."

He held perfectly still, half sure he'd misheard her. "Okay?"

"Yes." She tugged his shirt, towing him down to her. "We're meeting in the morning to discuss our next steps."

He carefully set his hands on her hips, relishing the ability to simply touch her like this. "Quite a few hours until then."

"Yes," she whispered.

He wanted nothing more than to rip her clothes off her and fuck her until the sun crested the horizon. To lose themselves in cementing this fledgling relationship. Because that's what it fucking was, whether she'd put a label on it or no. A relationship. There was no one else for Tristan, and he'd wait as long as it took for Amarante to settle into that truth.

But they needed to survive the coming confrontation first, and that meant he couldn't let his baser impulses ride shotgun. Amarante needed to be at the top of her game—they both did—and going into tomorrow exhausted would be a mistake.

"Come on." He forced himself to step back and take her hand. He could do this. He could take care of Amarante, could prove that he was here for *her*, not just for what she could give him. In the end, it really was that simple. He led her into her bathroom, ignoring her amused expression, and turned on the shower. "Wash. Sleep. Fuck in the morning."

Amarante released his hand and started undressing. "Interesting plan."

"It's a good plan." He sounded defensive, but he couldn't help it. Not with her stripping in smooth, economical movements right in front of him. She stepped out of her pants and walked into the shower without even looking at him. "It's a good plan," he repeated.

"Are you trying to convince me... or yourself?" She ducked beneath the spray, and his mouth went dry at the way the water coursed down her body.

Tristan fumbled out of his clothes and followed her into the shower. He couldn't stop his body's reaction, but he *could* ignore it. Damn it, he was determined to ignore it.

But Amarante turned around and stepped into him, sliding her hands up his chest and looping her arms around his neck. "I propose a compromise."

He clutched her to him. He couldn't help it. Fuck, she felt good, all slippery and restlessly shifting against him. "What kind of compromise."

She rolled her hips, pressing herself against his cock. "We fuck in the shower. We sleep. We fuck again in the morning. Then we plan our attack."

"You're killing me, Te."

"That's not the point of this endeavor." She nipped his jaw. "I'm being reasonable."

"Are you on birth control?"

She went still. "Yes. It seemed prudent, if not necessary."

Thank fuck for that. He leaned back so he could see her face. "I get tested regularly, but I'm not reckless with that shit. If you want—"

"I do." Her lips curled. "Take me, Tristan. Now."

Yeah, right. As if he was going to waste this opportunity with a quickie. Tristan guided her around and pressed her hands to the cool tile wall. He'd already scoped out the room while he waited for her, so he knew one of the shower heads detached. The others poured warm water over them as he reached above her head for it. He pressed against her back, holding her steady, and angled the water toward her clit. A small adjustment and she jerked against him. "Oh god."

He held steady as she shook, her hips rolling back against his cock, seeking him. "Not yet."

"I can't. I—" She came hard, her fingers clawing at the smooth tile. Tristan looped an arm around her waist to keep her on her feet and replaced the shower head. Amarante lolled back against him. "What the hell was that?"

"Warm up."

She laughed hoarsely. "Zero to sixty is not warm up. It's practically the main event."

"Then you get two main events tonight. Lucky you." He moved back enough that he could guide his cock into her. One smooth stroke and he was sheathed to the hilt. She gave a moan that he felt in his balls. Tristan cursed. "We get together and I'm in danger of coming in thirty seconds like some asshole sixteen-year-old."

"Mmm." She began moving, sliding him nearly all the way out and slamming back onto his cock. "Your lack of control is noted."

He gripped her hips, following her rhythm. It felt good. Too good. The kind of perfection that meant something terrible would show up on its heels. But that was tomorrow. Tonight, he had Amarante and the promise of a new beginning of sorts.

Tristan would fight tooth and nail to ensure the promise flourished into reality. He meant it when he said he'd never give her up again. If he had to fight the entire world in order to keep her safe and stand at her side, he'd do it and willingly.

Amarante came again, and the combination of his name on her lips and her pussy clamping around him threw him over the edge. He pounded into her, chasing his pleasure to completion. He braced one arm on the tile to keep them on their feet. "Feel better?"

She laughed, low and sinful. "I won't lie. It helped."

"Good." He shifted back and they both quickly cleaned off and finished up their shower. Tristan turned off the water and Amarante stepped out.

She shot him a look. "Don't you dare try to dry me off."

"Call it pampering."

"I won't call it anything of the sort." She threw a fluffy white towel that he barely caught in time. "I don't need a caretaker, Tristan."

He knew that. Of course he knew that. Amarante was the strongest person he knew, and she was more than capable of carrying the world around on her shoulders. It didn't mean she should have to, though. He knew better than to say as much aloud, though. He simply dried off and went through the motions of getting ready for bed beside her.

It was enough.

For now.

CHAPTER 21

*a*marante wasn't sure what she expected after they finished getting ready for bed, but it wasn't for Tristan to climb into bed with her. He tucked himself around her from the back and pressed a kiss to her neck. "Sleep."

Sleep? How was she supposed to sleep with him here, let alone touching her? She blinked into the darkness. "I'm not really a cuddler."

"Do you want me to move?"

Did she? She didn't know. That was the problem with Tristan. So many of her truths shifted when he entered the room. She thought she had things down, and then he'd say or do something and she'd question the very fabric of the universe. She *didn't* cuddle. When she and Cora spent time together, they invariably parted ways not too long after the fact. Cora had places to be, and neither of them wanted to deal with their respective siblings getting wind of their complicated friendship. The thought of Wrath knocking on her door made her shudder. She had enough trouble without borrowing that.

Tristan smoothed a hand down her side. "Do you want me to leave?"

"No." That, at least, was the truth. She rolled to face him. "I don't want you to leave. I just don't have a frame of reference for having you in my life. Fucking and plotting is one thing. Sleeping together is different."

He nodded slowly. "What do you need from me?"

A time machine, ideally. Even as scarred emotionally as she was a kid, she'd still been innocent in some ways. She and Tristan had done any number of things required to stay alive, but with each other there was an almost precious innocence. Neither of them had that shine anymore. "I don't know."

He gave her a half smile. "If you ever land on an answer, let me know."

"I will." This was wrong. It felt awkward and strange and she was so tense, she might shatter. On impulse, Amarante moved forward and pressed her face to Tristan's neck. She inhaled the faintest traces soap on his skin and, beneath that, the scent of the man himself. He immediately draped his arm over her hip. This wasn't so bad. She could relax into this...

Amarante opened her eyes to find herself alone in her bed.

She sat up and pushed her hair back from her face. A quick glance at the clock confirmed that it was well past six in the morning. She'd slept through the night. She climbed slowly to her feet. If not for the faint ache in her body, she could almost convince herself that last night had been a fever dream, that she hadn't walked into her room to find Tristan on her bed.

The bathroom door opened and the man himself emerged. "Morning, sunshine."

"Stop that."

He grinned around his toothbrush. "Stop what?"

"Stop being so…" She waved her hand vaguely in his direction. "Tone it down until I'm fully awake."

"As my lady commands." He disappeared back through the doorway, and she heard the sink running.

Amarante closed her eyes. There was so much hanging in the balance. She needed to ensure she was fully present so they could plan accordingly. Unfortunately, before they could get down to business, she'd have to deal with her siblings' reactions to Tristan. She couldn't very well let Kenzie or one of her brothers kill him. Not now. Not ever.

With a muffled sigh, she got ready. A quick shower. Makeup. Clothing. She skipped the reinforced clothing since they were on the Island of Ys. The only time Amarante dressed like that was during the Wild Hunt, when both enemies and allies came close to compete. No one had tried to slip a dagger between her ribs yet, but she'd be foolish not to take precautions.

By the time she finished, she found Tristan on her bed, flipping through one of the many novels she had stashed on the small bookcase next to the bed. He spoke without looking up. "Young Adult, huh I'm surprised."

He hadn't exactly asked for an explanation, but she gave one anyways. "Good always conquers evil in those stories. There's always a fight, always losses, but the main character always prevails."

He chewed on that for a moment and shut the book. "I retract my earlier statement." He finally looked at her and whistled. "Damn, Te. I didn't realize how into menswear I was until about a week ago."

She willed herself not to blush. Tristan could be charming when he wanted to be, and he obviously wanted to be right now. Whether it was to put her at ease before the coming confrontation or for darker motives, she couldn't be sure.

No, that was a lie.

She couldn't keep pretending she didn't trust him. He'd had her life in his hands half a dozen times. If he wanted to kill her, she'd be dead by now. Twice now, she'd slept at his side, completely defenseless. She couldn't even pretend she thought Zhao had sent him at this point. Zhao didn't give a fuck what she planned, because he had his own plans in place. With the might of his people, plus the other three families, they would win. There was little Amarante could do to fortify the island against that kind of attack, and even if she and the others ran, there were few places they could disappear to that didn't put them dangerously close to an enemy. He'd be focused on moving against them as quickly as possible.

She had to make sure she moved first.

"It's time."

Instantly, the amusement disappeared from his face. He rose and moved to stand in front of her. "We'll figure this out and kill the bastard before he has a chance to hurt anyone."

"Anyone else." Her chest felt too tight. "He's hurt far too many people already."

Tristan nodded slowly. "Anyone else."

"Let's go." The impulse to take his hand rose, and she couldn't stop herself from doing exactly that. The small touch grounded her in a way she didn't know how to deal with. But then, Tristan had always grounded her. It was one of the reasons she'd valued his company so much. He saw her, looked past the carefully curated mask to understand the strengths and weaknesses beneath. In all this time, he'd never once flinched away from her truth. She couldn't say that about anyone else, not even her siblings. At one point or another, they'd seen the depths she was capable of and turned away. Never for good, but it was enough to remind her that she stood apart. That she would always stand apart.

Tristan didn't allow that distance.

She kept a hold on his hand and led the way to the hub. Everyone was already there, all six of their expanded family. Amarante stopped in the doorway, Tristan at her side, and waited for the inevitable confrontation.

Kenzie saw him first. She blinked those big amber eyes and burst into motion. A blade appeared in her hand though Amarante had barely seen her move to grab it. She started to step in front of Tristan, to block his sister's attack, but he nudged her aside. It all happened in the space of a heartbeat.

Then Kenzie reached them and struck. Tristan dodged her first attack, and then her next. He pulled a move Amarante had seen before, grabbing her sister's wrist and sending the knife clattering across the floor. "I'm here to help."

"The fuck you are." Kenzie tried to knee him in the balls, but he turned at last moment and she nailed his thigh instead.

Tristan grabbed her arm and yanked her toward him, twisting and flipping her onto the couch. He'd aimed it perfectly. A foot to the right and she would have taken out the table and injured herself.

Luca started to stand, but Cami threw herself into his lap. "No."

"He just—"

"Luca *look*." She grabbed his chin and pointed his face toward Amarante. "If your sister didn't kill him the second he showed up, there's a reason."

Amarante raised her brows when Luca scowled. She'd been iffy on Cami when he first fell for the princess, but the woman had proved her skills and smarts time and time again. She'd read the situation correctly in seconds and moved to ensure Luca didn't aggravate his healing injury.

While she'd been distracted with that little drama, Ryu pulled a gun from the holster beneath his desk. He pointed it at Tristan's chest. "Give me one good reason not to pull the trigger."

Tristan carefully raised his hands. "I can help you get Zhao."

"That's not good enough." He shifted to stand in front of Delilah, who looked shocked by this turn of events and the flurry of violence that followed it.

This was getting out of hand. Amarante moved to stand in front of Tristan. "That's enough."

"Te, you can't be serious." He didn't take his gaze from Tristan. "Move out of the way."

She held up a hand, stopping Kenzie from charging again. "We have a limited time to strike before we're wiped off the map. Not just us—the entire island. There are too many lives on the line to let petty things get in the way."

"Petty things." Ryu glared. "He used threats against Delilah's sister to blackmail her. He scared the shit out of her."

She stared until he slowly lowered the gun. "I'm not going to defend his past actions. You can hash it out at another time. Right now, the bottom line is more important than anything in the past. We *have* to take Zhao out and take him out now." She motioned to Tristan over her shoulder. "He can help us."

"Prove it." This from Luca, who had finally gotten around Cami acting as a petite human barricade. He didn't move to attack, but he looked just as pissed at the others. "What you know is worth your life. So tell us."

Tristan touched Amarante's hip, a tiny nudge that got her moving. Every single eye in the room focused on his hand on her hip. Her skin prickled, but she ignored it and ignored their blatant shock. As she told them all, there would be time to deal with the implications of Tristan's presence later. Or they would all be dead and the future wouldn't matter. She stopped in front of the table that used to be big enough for her entire family to sit around it. Now, with their number doubled, it feel laughably small. It felt *sad*.

Maybe this wasn't a good idea. She'd intended to take on Zhao herself, and doing that still made sense. Her siblings had their entire lives ahead of them, the future now something than inspired hope instead of fear. For fuck's sake, Luca and Cami wanted to start a family. She couldn't ask them to risk it all for this.

"Yes, you can."

She hadn't realized she spoke aloud until Luca answered her. He stood across the table, Cami tucked against his side, his dark eyes serious. "This is our home, our life, our family that he's threatening. We have as much right to protect it as you do, Te. If anyone should sit this fight out, it's you. You've already paid too high a price for our safety." His gaze flicked to Tristan and away. She knew he'd suspected that she had someone back when they were teenagers, but he'd never directly asked her and she'd never offered the information.

Kenzie planted her hands on the table to Amarante's right. "If you even *think* about taking off without us again, I'm going to chase you down and hog-tie you and throw you in a trunk until this is all over. Luca's right. It's our fight. You might have been the one to make decisions for us when we were younger, but that's over now. We're either equals or we're not."

"You are," she said. Of course they were. Her wanting to protect them had nothing to do with her feelings on how capable they were. "I never thought of you as anything else."

"Then start acting like it."

She started to argue, but there was no point. Kenzie wasn't wrong and they had more important things to deal with right now. Tristan shifted next to her, his hand brushing her arm. A silent offer of support. He cleared his throat. "We'll need everyone to make this happen."

"You're expecting us to trust you." Ryu dropped into the chair to Amarante's left. "To put our lives in your hands."

"No," Amarante cut in before Tristan could respond. "I'm expecting you to trust *me*." That shut them up. All three of them looked at her with varying degrees of shock. She waited, but no one jumped up to say anything, so she motioned to Tristan. "Tell us your plan, and we'll consider it."

He shot her a grin. "Consider it. Cute." He straightened and it was like his amusing self dropped away. This Tristan was all business. "Zhao will have retreated to his compound. You can't hack your way in. There are over a hundred soldiers who sole purpose is to keep the bastard safe. You can't attack. They can stand a siege for years with the resources behind those walls."

"You aren't telling us anything we don't already know." Ryu reached back and covered Delilah's hand on his shoulder. For all the comforting move, his dark eyes were steady and intense. He always got like this when strategizing.

"What you don't know is that there's an escape route."

Amarante turned to look at him. "You're joking."

"I'm not." He shook his head. "He's too savvy to trap himself, even with all the resources he's spent ensuring the compound is unassailable."

But Kenzie was shaking her head. "This might have been useful information before you showed up, but he has to know you're here, which means he's going to ramp up whatever security he has on that route."

"Yes and no." Now Tristan did smile, but it was more a fierce baring of teeth than anything else. "No one knows about the route except Zhao himself. He's not the most trusting sort, and he'd be a fool to provide an enemy with a path straight to his back."

"Then how the hell do you know about it?"

"I like knowing things." Satisfaction rolled off him in waves. "Zhao doesn't know I know."

As tempting as it was to cling to that, Amarante shook her head. "We can't assume anything at this point. He's been playing a deeper game than anyone else without us realizing it. It's entirely possible that he had you watched the whole time you were there."

"Yes, it is possible. But Zhao tends to disappear anyone who steps out of line, and he had extra motivation to ensure I didn't know about it." Tristan shrugged. "I can be sneaky when I want to. "

Considering she'd found him in her room, and she still wasn't quite sure how he'd managed it. There were no other entrances except through the hub. They'd made sure of that when they built the place. Most of the public rooms could be accessed by the back halls through various means, but the hub only had one entrance and exit. Somehow Tristan had not only found the hub, but navigated it without any of them seeing him. It defied explanation. "I believe that," she muttered.

Ryu got to his feet and walked over to push a few buttoned on the nearest computer. The wall of monitors shifted to reveal a large map of Zhao's compound. It wasn't perfect; he'd pulled the satellite images and they'd made notes from there, all of which were on the image itself.

Tristan whistled and moved around the table to get a closer look. "You've done your homework."

"Show us where the secret entrance is. Now."

CHAPTER 22

*T*ristan was impressed with the level of detail the Horsemen had managed to divine about Zhao's compound. It wasn't perfect, but it was more comprehensive than he'd expected. *Good. That will make this easier.* He pointed to a spot about half a mile out in the trees to the south. "This is where the entrance is."

Ryu immediately moved to this computer again, a look of concentration on his face. He wouldn't be able to verify Tristan's claim, but he didn't fault the man for trying. Acting on his claims required a whole lot more trust than anyone but Amarante had in him. *He* wouldn't trust some asshole who showed up and started making claims, not unless he was backed against the wall without another option.

Which was exactly where the Horsemen were right now.

Luca pulled his woman onto his lap and stared at the wall of monitors. "We have no guarantee that going after Zhao directly will work."

"No." He wouldn't sugar-coat it for them. They already knew the truth, even if they fought against it. "But if you don't kill him and do it publicly, the other three families will align behind him and they'll wipe you off the map. Even if you evacuate, they'll likely send teams to take out your people. A full scale removal of anything connected with the Horsemen."

None of them jumped up to say that was bullshit or that it wouldn't happen. They'd been moving through this world as long as he had. They knew better.

Finally, Amarante moved, slipping her hands into her pockets. "We need to know where the entrance comes out inside the compound and a map of the area." She stared at the monitors. "We can't kill him in the compound. It's possible that someone will try to cover up his death, or downplay it. We have to take him with us and make an example of him."

He'd been afraid she was going to say that. "It's a bad idea."

"It's the only one that makes this level of risk worth it. We have to be sure no one will dare cross us in the future, and this is the only way." She didn't look at him. "And once he's dead, we go after the camp in a concentrated attack. Take out the adults. Free the children. Return the ones who have families they know about."

Kenzie looked at her sister, her pale complexion going a little green. "And the others?"

"I'm not sure yet. We're not equipped to deal with them here, though I suppose we'll have to give some of them the option. The older ones who have been there the longest will have a more difficult time integrating into something resembling a normal life." She blinked and shook her head. "But that's something to worry about after this hurdle."

She was already thinking ten steps ahead, and he loved her for it. Amarante blew his fucking mind over and over again, and just when he was sure they were two sides to the same damaged coin, she'd go and do something like this to prove that Bueller hadn't killed that softer side of her. She just hid it better than her siblings.

"The entrance is a carefully concealed metal hatch. It's a cement tunnel that leads to here." He moved around and pointed at a spot in the main building. "It's a storage closet on the first floor. If we strike at night, Zhao will likely be in his suite, which is on the third floor in the same building." He turned back to face them. "I'll draw you out a map. We can expect the guard schedule to be more intense than normal. He's confident no one can get to him, but he's also not stupid. He won't be taking any chances."

"If he was that smart, he'd weld the hatch shut." Kenzie gave him a sunny smile he didn't trust for a second. "But I suppose every rat wants a way out of a sinking ship if it comes to that."

Zhao was too paranoid to block off his failsafe means of escape. If he was willing to do that, he wouldn't have built it in the first place. But in all Tristan's time working in the compound, he'd never seen evidence that it was used. Which meant it was most likely exactly what it appeared to be—a last resort Zhao didn't want anyone but himself knowing about. "I need to be with the team that breaches the tunnel. I have Zhao's personal codes, and I know the place like the back of my hand."

Amarante and her siblings exchanged a look. Luca snorted. "You know, you don't sound much like the loyal man you're supposed to be."

"Because I'm not loyal to Zhao. I never have been." He held the other man's gaze. "I'm loyal to myself—and to Amarante."

Luca's brows dropped, but Amarante spoke before they could devolve back to fighting again. "We split into two groups. Luca and Kenzie and their partners will create a diversion on the north side. It has to look like a full scale attack, and it has to go on long enough to provide cover for Tristan, Ryu, and I to take the tunnel into the compound and retrieve Zhao." She glanced at the Latina woman standing at Ryu's back. "Delilah, you'll stay here and monitor communications to ensure everything goes off without a problem."

Smart. Delilah was an exotic dancer and while Tristan could attest to her operating well under pressure, to the best of his knowledge—and it was extensive—she didn't have any fighting or shooting skills. Out there, she'd be a liability, and her presence would make Ryu a liability as well. Keeping her back here was the best option.

Delilah opened her mouth, but Ryu squeezed her hand and spoke before she could. "Let's get this lined out."

As tempting as it was to try to lead, Tristan knew better. These four worked together like a well-oiled machine. It was what had kept them alive all these years, and it was what made them such formidable enemies. He noticed that the other partners did the same. Delilah moved into the kitchen area, put on a pot of coffee, and started digging through the fridge and laying ingredients out on the counter. Cami and Liam watched the planning closely, but they held themselves at the smallest distance away. They'd obviously gone through these kind of meetings before and knew it was best to simply follow orders.

Tristan dropped into a chair and watched as they went to work, answering whatever questions were fired his way. Luca shoved a pen and paper in his direction. "Draw the floor plan."

By the time he was done, they had a full scale plan. Kenzie, Luca, Cami, and Liam would use his knowledge to avoid patrols to get close and then they'd set off a series of flashy explosions near the north-east corner of the compound. While people were rushing to put out the inevitable fires, Luca and Cami would shift to the north-west section—directly opposite the escape tunnel—and open fire. Meanwhile, Kenzie and Liam would prey on the soldiers outside the walls, ramping up fear and making it seem like it was a full scale attack. If they could get a few of the soldiers to panic, it would put the entire compound on alert and would draw a significant number of Zhao's men to the north wall.

Which would leave the way south open for Tristan, Amarante, and Ryu.

It wasn't a full-proof plan by any means. Nothing about this was guaranteed. A thousand things could go wrong. It was still their best shot.

Amarante tapped her fingers on the table, her gaze a thousand miles away. "We bring him back here to the small island. I'll handle that, but it needs to be recorded. Afterward, Ryu will ensure the tape gets to the Romanovs, the Nakamuras, and the Prietos."

"It might not be enough." Tristan raised his brows when every eye in the room turned to him, most of them hostile. "I think it will make them scatter because of what a large player Zhao is, but there's a small possibility that they will continue with the alliance."

"Then we will make examples of them, too." Amarante spoke as if it was the simplest thing in the world. But she wasn't exactly wrong. Tristan operated in the same way: mow down his enemies until the rest were too scared to face him. As strategies went, it had a long history of success. She focused on him. "Do you have anything to add to this?"

"The sooner we move, the better." He didn't like rushing into this, but the longer they gave Zhao to work on the other three families, the greater the chance of an alliance surviving his death. Tristan didn't have an in with the other families the same way he did with Zhao. They'd be flying blind, and fuck if he was going to lose Amarante just when he found her again. "I'd estimate that you have less than a week before he works his magic on the others, maybe less."

"We leave tomorrow." Amarante pushed to her feet. "You four figure out what you need and stock up. We aren't going to have much in the way of transport, so you'll have to be able to carry it in and carry whatever is left out or be willing to leave it behind." She nodded at Tristan. "You're with me. Let's go."

He didn't ask questions. He just rose and followed her out of the hub. They wove through the narrow hallways until Amarante pushed a section of a wall and it opened to reveal a luxurious sitting room. It looked like something that belonged in a palace, where ladies got together to do whatever the fuck rich ladies did. He stepped into the room and watched Amarante shut the door. It clicked and then it was just another wall panel, totally indistinguishable from the rest. "The Warren has a lot of sneaky shit like this."

"Where do you think I got the idea from?" She gave him a sharp smile, but it fell from her lips almost immediately. "Tell me the truth, Tristan. Did Zhao send you?"

It stung that she still suspected him, though he couldn't blame her in the least. "No."

"Because if you're about to get my entire family killed, I —" She looked away, took a breath, and looked back. "Then I'll go alone. Now."

"You just got done telling Kenzie that you wouldn't go off half-cocked."

Her mouth thinned. "Better for me to die alone than to die with all of them at my side. You say you love me? Prove it. Tell me the truth."

Fuck, but she never ceased to amaze him. Tristan stepped closer and closer yet until she had to crane her neck back to hold his gaze. He carefully framed her face with his hands. "I'm not here on Zhao's orders. Or anyone's orders. He cut me loose, just like I told you. I haven't lied to you once since I got here."

She sighed. "That's quite the qualifier."

"It's the truth." He didn't know how to let down his barriers. Not when he'd spent so much time building them up to keep himself safe. With Amarante, though, he didn't have to. She was already inside with him. "I came here for you, Te. You're the one I choose. No one else."

"I really want to believe you right now."

He brushed his thumbs over her cheeks. "I don't believe in shit, so swearing on something won't mean a single damn thing. But I believe in us."

"Tristan."

"I swear on us that I'm telling the truth."

She closed her eyes for a long moment and he found himself holding his breath. Finally, Amarante sighed. "Okay."

"Okay?"

"Yeah, okay. Let's get moving." She stepped back carefully and he dropped his hands. If they survived this attack, then they could talk about the future. There was no point until they knew how things would fall out with Zhao.

Tristan followed Amarante out the back door he'd scoped out earlier. He'd ultimately chosen to sneak in through the front, initially hiding in plain sight before he found one of the doors into the secondary passageways he'd suspected existed. There was a small dock with an equally small boat tied to it. "Not exactly seaworthy."

"It doesn't have to be. We're just island hopping." She stepped easily into the tiny thing, looking strangely at home there despite her designer suit. Tristan followed more slowly. When he was settled on the plank across from her, she raised her brows. "You're not afraid of the water, are you?"

"Not afraid. I just have a healthy respect for settings where I'm not the apex predator." He jerked his thumb at the gorgeous blue stretching to the horizon. "The ocean tops the list."

"Finally. A tiny sign of humility." She turned the engine over and slowly steered them away from the dock.

Tristan tried to relax. Amarante never took them far from shore, hugging the island line as she took them south. He wasn't much on an outdoors type of guy, but even he could appreciate the beauty of this island. Even more, he could appreciate how she'd beat back nature to create a safe space of her own. "It's amazing what you've done with this place."

"I know."

He shot her a grin. "I'm not stroking your ego, Te. I mean it. Most of us just take and take and take from others. You went and created something new. It's impressive."

"It wasn't easy. But it's worth it." She veered away from the shoreline toward a tiny island directly south.

He'd noticed it, of course, but he'd thought it was one of the countless unoccupied island in this area off the coast of Africa. There were thousands of them, some housing resorts and residences, but most left to nature because they were too small or missing something necessary to support human life. Or maybe they were just too much of a pain in the ass to build on. He didn't know and he didn't give a fuck.

Another tiny dock awaited them, this one partially hidden in the rise of the rock. Rocks were weird here, giant rectangle formations that looked alien and strange. Amarante tied the boat off and climbed out easily. "This won't take long."

He still didn't know what *this* was, but he followed along. She had her reasons for being here, for bringing him here, and he doubted those reasons included answering half a dozen questions.

They headed up a small rise and down a barely tended path into the single copse of trees. He stopped short. There was a squat square building made of concrete. No windows. A single door. This was a jail cell if he'd ever seen one. Doubt rose, but he ignored it. Amarante either trusted him or she didn't. It was too late to do anything but walk through the door she opened and meet his fate.

Inside was both what he expected and not. Three doors with impressive electronic locks on them that he'd be hard-pressed to hack. A tile floor with a drain in the center. He looked up and noted the hooks in the ceiling. *Torture chamber.*

It lined up. Bueller held no end to atrocities, but Amarante's fate had been extra fucked up. They forced her to torture people for their amusement. Tristan fought back a shudder and kept his expression placid. "You should fire your interior designer."

"Always with the jokes." She shook her head and walked a slow circle around the room.

Despite himself, he asked, "What is this place, Te?"

She gave him an eerily empty smile. "This is where my father is going to die."

CHAPTER 23

*L*ess than twenty-four hours later, Amarante crouched in the darkness between Ryu and Tristan. They all wore uniform black gear and boots, the better to move with ease. A small, silly part of her missed her suits, but it would be the height of stupidity to go on a mission like this dressed as anything less than a solider.

Tristan peeled back a thick textured blanket-like thing to reveal a square metal hatch. If he hadn't been here to show them where it was, it would have taken hours to find. If they'd found it at all. He touched the locking mechanism on the center of it. "When they start the attack, we'll open it."

"There won't be alarms." The suspicion in Ryu's voice was warranted, but she appreciated that he'd put his issues with Tristan aside for the time being. She'd have to deal with them later if they all survived this, but *later* didn't exist in this moment.

"To have alarms means people would know about this." Tristan gently tapped the hatch. "And no one does. Zhao went so far as to kill the people who worked on it to ensure no word got out."

Her brother's face twisted. "And yet somehow you found it. You can't seriously expect us to believe that."

"Believe what you want. It took me seven years of haunting that fucking place to realize the storage closet was more than it seemed and another three to get all the codes I needed to work this."

That kind of dedication staggered her if she thought about it too hard. Not that Tristan had the patience to play the long game; she had that kind of patience and more. No, it was that he'd remained in Zhao's household for so long while actively collecting information that may or may not have been of use down the road. He had no guarantees at any point. "Would you have stayed?"

He didn't ask her to elaborate. "I don't know. If I'd found out about the camp sooner... No. He made sure to keep it from me, and he was damn careful about it, too. So it's possible I might not have if you didn't force his hand." He shrugged. "I don't know."

Not the answer she wanted, but a truthful one all the same.

Amarante's body hummed with adrenaline. Waiting was the worst part. Once they moved, she could put all this pent up energy into action. "No mistakes."

"No mistakes," they repeated.

The first explosion tore through the night. She couldn't see it from her position, but it sounded like someone had dropped a bomb on the other side of the compound. A second. A third. "What the hell did they put in those things?"

Ryu chuckled. "When it comes to Kenzie, it's better not to ask."

Tristan touched the numbers quickly and she held her breath as they waited for the lock to click open. The second it did, he wrenched the hatch up. "Let's go."

Ryu went first, disappearing into the hole without a

word. Amarante cast a long look at Tristan and followed her brother down the metal ladder into darkness. Tristan came last, carefully leaving the hatch open behind them. They'd argued about the best option there, but ultimately closing it made no sense because they couldn't afford to leave someone behind to cover it again. Better to have their exit route open and hope like hell that no one stumbled across it in the meantime.

With the explosions still rocking the night, it was a pretty good bet that it'd be fine when they got back. As long as they hurried.

She touched her headlamp to turn it on, fighting back the darkness. Ryu and Tristan did the same. Tristan's hand brushed hers as he carefully maneuvered to the front of their little line. "Let's get this done."

They wasted no energy speaking as they traversed the dark tunnel. She couldn't shake the feeling of dankness, despite the concrete walls being perfectly dry. Maybe it was being underground that tricked her mind. She didn't know. Instead of looking around, Amarante focused on the circle of light her headlamp created on Tristan's back. The steady beat of his feet in front of her and Ryu's behind her. A slow count to one hundred and they reached a second ladder.

"Lights off," Tristan murmured.

She didn't want to, but she ignored the tiny whimper of fear. It had no place here. Giving in meant death, and *she* was the only death who stalked these halls. Amarante clicked off her light and Ryu did the same behind her, letting darkness flood in until she couldn't see anything at all.

They stood there and listened to Tristan climb the ladder. Ryu's hand found hers in the dark and she squeezed it, trying very, very hard not to think back to another time many years ago, when they stood shoulder to shoulder in the dark. He'd been crying then. She'd been terrified. Neither of them knew what waited for them, only that they'd been hauled from their beds in the middle of the night by masked figures.

Neither of them had any idea that their father was the one who'd ordered it.

And she still didn't know *why*.

"Clear." Tristan's voice floated down from above, barely more than a whisper.

Ryu squeezed her hand one last time and released her. Amarante hated how shaky she felt as she climbed the ladder. This wasn't supposed to be a weak moment, and she had no time for these inconvenient feelings from her childhood rising beneath her skin.

Get in. Get Zhao. Get out. That was all that mattered.

The ladder ended and she blindly reached up to find the doorway. There was nothing but wall. *What the hell?*

"Behind you," Tristan murmured. Then his hands were there, hooking her around the waist and hauling her back into the storage closet.

The scent of dust assailed her nose and she had to concentrate hard to keep from sneezing. A few moments later, Tristan helped Ryu into the closet, too. The space was nowhere near large enough for the three of them, so it took some jostling and awkwardness before he was able to slide the back wall shut. He flicked on his head lamp on the lowest setting. "This is how you open it." He took her hand and pressed it to a slight irregularity on the left side of the wall. It gave with a tiny click and the wall moved. "Got it?"

She didn't ask why he wanted to show her. It was in case something happened to Tristan before they got out of there. Amarante opened her mouth to tell him that she wouldn't leave him behind, no matter what, but he pressed a finger to her lips. "Get out safely, Te. That's all I ask."

"Let's go," Ryu said softly.

He went out the door first and Amarante followed close behind, with Tristan bringing up the rear. The hallway was empty, but they could hear gunshots and yelling in the distance. The others were still keeping up their distraction. She checked her watch. "We have ten minutes. Maybe less."

"This way." Tristan headed down the hallway.

Amarante followed, trying not to pay too much attention to the art lining the walls. She'd never set foot in this compound, had been born in a different home in a different part of China, but it felt the same. She hadn't been prepared for that, but she should have been. Zhao showed every sign of being a creature of habit. Of course his sense of style would stretch forward to this point.

Tristan took them up a set of stairs to the third floor. "He'll be through here." He glanced at them. "Are you ready?"

No. Not in the least. And yet as ready as she would ever be. She glanced at Ryu and wasn't surprised to find him just as pale as she felt. They nodded at each other. "We're ready."

"Okay." He didn't ask again, which she appreciated. He simply headed to a massive set of doors at the end of the short hallway. Amarante barely had time to brace before Tristan threw them open. He swept left and Ryu swept right, leaving her to handle the rest of the room. She took in the massive space. A desk, a bed, a fireplace large enough to stand in, all dripping opulence.

Empty.

Ryu shut the doors behind them and Tristan headed for the bathroom. It was only then that she heard water running. She exchanged a look with her brother. Zhao was in the shower. *Really?* It seemed too good to be true. Which meant it must be. "Tristan, wait."

Too late.

He opened the bathroom door and a gunshot rang out.

Tristan stumbled back and fell to the ground, his hand to his shoulder. "Fuck!"

Zhao emerged, fully dressed and holding a gun. "Weapons on the ground."

Amarante shot before he had a chance to finish speaking. Her bullet took him in the fleshy part of his bicep. He hit the wall and the gun hit the floor. Tristan kicked it away. The whole thing had taken seconds, though she was breathing like she'd just run a marathon. "Ryu, tie his hands and bandage that wound. I don't want him bleeding out until I'm ready."

Zhao tried to fight, but Ryu delivered a vicious punch to his jaw. While he was stunned, her brother zip-tied his hands in front of him and tore off several strips of sheets. Two went around Zhao's bicep. The others, he handed to Amarante.

She knelt next to Tristan. "That was a stupid thing to do."

"Brave."

"Same thing." She started to peel his shirt away from the wound, but he grabbed her wrist. Amarante glared. "If you bleed to death, I'm going to kill you myself."

"A bit redundant, Te." His voice was off, strained from pain. He took the strips of sheets from her, wadded them up, and stuffed them down his shirt to where his holster kept them in place. "I'll hold."

"Tristan—"

"I'll hold. Let's go. We don't have much time."

Time. She had no idea how much they had left. Amarante helped him to his feet and turned to find Ryu with Zhao over his shoulder. Her brother looked like he might be sick, but he locked it down when he caught her eye. "I'm fine. Let's get out of here."

"Without a hitch," she murmured.

Amarante led the way out of the suite and back down the

hall. She couldn't heard explosions anymore, and only the occasional sound of gunfire. They were running out of time. Three steps down the stairs and she froze. "Someone's coming." Several sets of footsteps sounded below. She reached for her gun. The goal was sneak in and sneak out without a confrontation. The three of them couldn't hold against the kind of numbers Zhao had in this place. Every minute they were held up decreased the likelihood of them getting out of here alive.

"I've got this." Tristan moved to stand on the stair next to her. "I'll hold them off long enough for you to get him out. You'll be moving slower with his unconscious ass and you'll need the extra time."

His words refused to make sense in her mind. "You can't seriously be asking me to leave you."

"I'm not asking you shit, Te. I'm telling you that I'll carve you out a window." He snagged the back of her neck and towed her in for a quick kiss. "Get you and your family out of here. I'll catch up."

If they left without him, there would be no catching up. There would only be his death. "I'm not leaving you."

"You don't have a choice." He moved faster than he had right to, shoving her back. She landed on her ass, but by the time she scrambled to her feet, Tristan was gone, disappearing down the stairs.

She started after him, but Ryu's voice stopped her short. "We have to go."

"I'm not leaving him."

"Te." He waited for her to look at him. "I can't get Zhao out of here on my own."

Indecision ripped through her. Every instinct she had demanded she go after Tristan, to ensure he stayed safe. To lose him was unthinkable… But they were so close to their goal. She couldn't fail her family. Her breath sawed out in a sound suspiciously like a sob. She had no choice. "Come on."

They made it back to the storage closet without seeing a single person, but the sound of gunshots echoed through the house. Tristan, holding off Zhao's men, creating a distraction, acting in penance? She didn't know. She was desperately afraid she'd never get a chance to ask him.

The drop from the door to the bottom of the tunnel was barely six feet. Ryu hung Zhao by his arms and dropped him. The impact woke the older man up, and his curses filled the closed space as they climbed down. Amarante turned on her head lamp and stared at him. This man had seemed almost larger than life when she faced off with him in the Warren. Down here in the dark, his truth was revealed. "You're just a man."

Ryu stopped short and looked at her strangely. "What?"

"Zhao." She stood over him. "For so long you were the bogeyman who haunted the darkness, the evil thing that would kill us if we stepped out of line. And then you were the enemy, which made you larger still. In reality, you're none of those things. You are a man who is selfish and greedy and evil yes, but just a man."

"Te, we have to keep moving if we're going to get him out of here."

"We're not getting him out of here." All her plans, her carefully detailed tortures... What was the point? She wouldn't get the answers she craved because there *were* no answers. Nothing he could say would justify what he'd done. No information she could pull from him would change the people she and her siblings had become because of the evil he allowed to flourish in that place. Leaving with him would cut her off from one of the few things she actually cared about in this world. The price was too high. She wouldn't do it. "Get out of here, Ryu."

"*What?*"

"I'll take care of Zhao, and then I'm going back for Tristan."

Zhao let out a wet laugh. "He's mine more than he's yours, girl. He was from the moment I offered him a chance away from you."

So much hate, and for what?

It didn't matter. Sometimes hate existed simply because it was. Zhao hated her, and she suspected he always had. Why else send his own children to that place? No one sane did such things, and there wasn't a single reasoning that would make sense when held up to the light. "He was always mine, Zhao." She purposefully stepped on the bend of his elbow and crouched down to grip his wrist. "I'm simply taking back what's mine now. My man, my life, my birthright." She wrenched on his wrist and he cried out as the bones broke.

As soon as his scream faded, he started talking again. "Your birthright? Don't make me laugh. My people will never accept *you*."

"Te, what are you doing?"

She ignored her brother, but Zhao turned hateful dark eyes in Ryu's direction. "They won't accept you, either. Weak, both of you. Pathetically weak."

"They don't have to accept me." She moved to his other side and repeated the process, faster this time. Amarante barely waited for him to stop cursing to continue. "I'm going to dismantle everything you built. Everything you worked so hard to accomplish. It will all be ash in the wind when I'm through. No one will remember your name."

"You don't have the balls."

"I don't need the balls. I am Death." She broke first one knee and then the other. There. He wouldn't be climbing any ladders ever again. "I had plans for you, Zhao, but this has a certain poetic justice. A paranoid evil man dying in the very escape route he created, the one no one knows about but him." She smiled down at him. "You may scream. I'm told that the concrete will muffle sound so I doubt anyone will hear you."

"You *bitch*."

She turned to her brother. "Get out of here and meet the others. I'm going back for him."

"You can't honestly expect me to leave you."

"I do." She pulled him into a rough hug. "I have no intention of dying today, but if we're not back to the rendezvous point by dawn, leave without us."

"Te—"

"Please do this for me. Delilah is waiting for you. Your *future* is waiting for you. Please don't argue with me right now."

He hesitated, but finally nodded. "Go get your man."

"I intend to." She stood there and watched her brother and then the light of his head lamp disappear into the darkness. Amarante breathed out the tiniest sigh of relief. She hadn't been sure Ryu would listen to her.

"You're not going to ask me why?"

She turned back to the man on the ground. Fear finally showed in those dark eyes, a true understanding that he wouldn't be getting out of this situation alive, that he had a very long, very painful death ahead of him. It was nothing more than he deserved. She stepped over him and headed for the ladder. "No, Zhao. I'm not going to ask you why. The 'why' doesn't matter. It doesn't change what happened to me —to us—and it doesn't change what we became. I don't care about your reasons."

"I made you what you are! You should be on your knees thanking me!"

She ignored him and climbed the ladder, his increasingly frantic words following her. He would die in the dark with terror consuming him. It wasn't anywhere near enough to balance the scales of what he'd done, but nothing was. She would do exactly what she promised. She would dismantle everything he'd built, even if it took the rest of her life to do it.

First, though, she had the love of her life to save.

CHAPTER 24

*T*ristan wasn't getting out of this alive.

He'd suspected as much when he kissed Amarante, but a part of him had still held out hope that he could make this work. Now, pinned down in the hallway, he had to face the truth. He had a single clip left and there were more men coming by the minute. Amarante's siblings' distraction was over, and now everyone would pour back into this building as wave after wave of reinforcements arrived.

Not to mention that he was starting to feel light headed from the bullet in his shoulder. They didn't have to out-shoot him. They just had to wait for blood loss to do its work and he'd pass out.

Fuck.

A canister flew down the hallway... from the wrong direction. He stared at it as it sailed past him. Seconds later, gas filled the space. Tristan covered his mouth, but it was no use. It coated his throat and stung his eyes. Damn it, they'd flanked him. He had to find a way out of this spot before it turned into a kill box. A figure appeared out of the gas and he tried to raise his gun, but they moved too fast, slamming their foot down on his wrist and pinning to the ground. They crouched down and lifted the mask and surely blood loss was making him see things because no way was Amarante here. "What the hell?"

"Stop wasting time with stupid questions." She moved off his hand and shoved a gas mask at him. "We have to move."

It really was her.

He yanked the mask over his face, exhaling in relief that quickly turned to anger. What the *fuck* was she doing here? She should be off Zhao property by now, safely en route to her island. "Amarante—"

"No time." She disappeared back through the smoke, and he had no choice but to follow her.

She must have studied the map he drew more closely than he'd realized, because she led him unerringly through the halls toward the side door. They passed a dozen bodies as they ran. Her handiwork, obviously. Fuck, but she was something else.

Amarante tore her mask off. "We have to hurry. We don't want to be trapped by the fires I set."

Fires. Now that she mentioned it, he could see a faint haze of smoke. "I love you."

"I know." She gave him a brief smile, but it faded as she took in his shirt, wet with blood. "Stay on your feet until I get you out of here. You can pass out later, but if I have to carry you, we're both going to die."

"I won't pass out." His body threatened to make a liar of him, his head woozy and his movements slower than normal. It didn't matter. Against all reason, she'd come back for him. He'd do whatever it took to ensure she got out of this alive. No matter the cost. "Zhao?"

"Later." She opened the side door and something whooshed deeper in the house. Amarante shoved him out into the night. "We have a lot of ground to cover and not much time. Come on."

Two guards came running around the side of the building. Tristan fumbled for his gun, but he shouldn't have bothered. Amarante took them down in a single shot each. "What are you waiting for, a written invitation? *Move.*"

He moved.

They rushed through the compound to the wall and started working their way to the only entrance and exit. The front gates. He didn't know how the fuck they would make it through. No matter how many people she took down, there were always more, and the gates would hold a concentrated number. The distraction early worked against them now. He was about to say as much when a rumble tore through the night. "What the fuck?"

Behind them, an entire section of the wall blew inward. The force of the explosion took out the small building in front of it and knocked Tristan back a few steps. Amarante steadied him with her body at his back. "Looks like we have a better option, though I'm going to kick their ass when we get out of here."

Understanding dawned. Her siblings. Obviously, she'd given them the same command he'd given her—with identical results. "Be a shame not to use the exit they just made us."

"I agree." She shot him a look. "You with me?"

"I'm with you." In every way that counted.

He forced his body into motion, following her back to the giant hole in the wall. Rubble shifted beneath his feet, threatening to topple him, but sheer willpower kept him moving despite how lightheaded he was. They charged out of the hole to find one of the trucks that they'd driven in with waiting for them, Ryu behind the wheel. Luca and Kenzie crouched in the bed, guns in hand. Kenzie saw them and the relief on her face was plain to see. "Stop playing coy and get the fuck in here!"

Amarante shoved Tristan into the truck first and then hauled herself in after him. "Go."

Ryu didn't hesitate to obey. He floored it, sending them hurtling down the narrow gap between the wall and the trees. It wasn't meant to be a road, but that didn't stop him. He turned the corner and gunshots sounded—Kenzie and Luca firing at the men still on the walls. Then they hit the actual road and picked up speed. In seconds, the compound disappeared behind them.

"That was really fucking stupid, Te." Ryu white-knuckled the steering wheel, his angry gaze on the road. "You promised you wouldn't."

She glanced at Tristan, her expression going soft. "I couldn't leave him."

"Damn it." Ryu shook his head. He leaned forward to pin Tristan with a look. "You are *not* who I would have chosen for my sister, but…" He shook his head. "Welcome to the fucked up family."

Tristan hadn't expected this. He hadn't expected *any* of this. "You were supposed to leave."

She twisted to face him. "We need to get this shirt off you and see how bad the wound is."

"Not until we reach the plane." Ryu took a turn too fast. "We have medical equipment there. He's still conscious so he'll hold until then. Probably."

Tristan ignored Ryu and caught Amarante's hand. "You were supposed to leave," he repeated.

She turned her hand to lace her fingers through his. "You should know better by now, Tristan. I protect those I love. I was never leaving you behind." She frowned down at him. "Don't you dare die before we get you medical attention."

"Yes, ma'am." Despite his best efforts, though, darkness ate at the edges of his vision and sucked him under.

* * *

AMARANTE DIDN'T LEAVE Tristan's side as they carted him into the plane and she and Cami got started patching him up. The bullet wound was a through and through, which was the only thing that had gone right today. He must have passed out from blood loss, but he'd be okay as long as nothing else went wrong. They had to strap him down while the plane took off, but she breathed a little sigh of relief as they reached cruising altitude.

It was done.

She glanced over to find her siblings watching her. *Not quite done yet.* It took more effort than it should have to release Tristan's limp hand and move away from him. Liam and Cami took one look at her face and went to Tristan's side. They weren't quite out of earshot, but she appreciated the attempt at privacy.

She took the empty chair next to Ryu, across from the backward facing chairs with Kenzie and Luca. Kenzie opened her mouth, but it was Ryu who spoke. "Why?"

She was suddenly terrified that nothing she said would make sense. Amarante swallowed hard. "In that tunnel, I had to make a choice. The past or the future. I chose the future."

Luca didn't blink. "Did you get the answers you wanted?" They weren't answers he needed. He'd been stolen from his family's home in Thalania. Kenzie's history was more ambiguous. She didn't remember her family or anything before Bueller. Ryu and Amarante were the only ones betrayed on so many levels by the very person who was supposed to keep them safe.

She turned to Ryu. "Is there any answer he could have given that would change what happened to us?"

"No."

"I thought there could be." She shook her head. "Down there, I realized the truth. It doesn't matter why. He doesn't get credit for what we became. We did it despite him. All four of us." She gave a grim smile. "And he will die a slow and painful death in the dark of the tunnel he built for selfish needs."

Kenzie matched her smile. "You're scary, but I like it." She let the expression drop. "It feels like it's not enough, though."

"That's because it's not." Amarante drummed her fingers on the armrest. "I fully intend to systematically dismantle every branch of his operations—starting with the replacement camp. It could take years, though."

Ryu have her a long look. "I think you mean *we* intend to systematically dismantle every branch of his operations."

"I can't ask anyone else to start a new journey like this when we just finished the last."

Luca snorted. "Te, give us some credit. Did you think we were going to be sitting on our asses and sipping fruity drinks for the rest of our lives? That's not how we work. That's not how we're ever going to work."

"You're starting a family."

His tan complexion went red. "Yeah, well, balance is the key to life. We can have the good, too. Even if it's dangerous, it's ours. We're more than capable of handling anything that comes our way." He held her gaze. "Together."

"Together," Ryu and Kenzie echoed.

A tension she hadn't realized she carried dissipated at their words. She sank back into the seat and sighed. "There is one last thing."

"Tristan." Ryu scrubbed his hands over his face. "You *would* fall for that charming psychopath."

"We have a long history."

Luca chuckled. "I expect you'll get more than your fair share of shit after all the hoops you made us jump through to get our happily ever afters. But I'm happy for you, Te. Truly."

"God, we're going sappy in our old age." Kenzie leaned forward and yanked Amarante into a hug. "Yes, yes, we're happy for you. But I think all these changes are going to require some construction on Pleasure to expand the hub. We passed *cozy* three people ago."

Warmth spread through Amarante's chest. "I think we can make that happen."

"Amarante."

She glanced over her shoulder. Cami smiled. "He's awake."

Just like that, she was on her feet. The others spread out throughout the plane, and Ryu took out his phone, no doubt to call Delilah. Satisfied that all was as it should be, Amarante sank into the seat next to the cot Tristan was strapped to. He narrowed those blue eyes at her. "I told you to go on without me."

"I did." She smiled, feeling strangely loopy. "I came back to save you from yourself. Were you planning on bleeding out in the hallway in some kind of noble death? I have to say, I expected better from you."

"I was considering my options." He held out his hand and she linked her fingers through his. "Where is he?"

No need to ask which *he* Tristan meant. "How sound-proof do you think that tunnel is?"

Understanding flared across his features. "Probably not perfect, but there will be a whole hell of a lot of activity for the next few days while they deal with the damage and repairs. As long as he can't climb out..."

"He can't."

"Then I don't expect he'll have enough strength to be

heard when things finally settle down." He searched her face. "Will that be enough?"

There was no room for anything but honesty here. "No. But the next few years of burning everything he ever cared about to ash will. Considering the truly evil things he's been involved in, I expect it will balance out both our karmic debts and then some."

He traced an abstract pattern on her knuckles. "I know a guy with some useful information if you're willing. He's got more than his fair share of karmic debt to balance out." He lifted their linked hands and pressed a kiss to her knuckles. "And he loves the fuck out of you."

"Sounds like my kind of guy." She had a hard time catching her breath. "I love you. I never stopped, even when I hated you. If you want, there's a spot on the Island of Ys for you."

He watched her closely. "Is that spot next to you?"

"Yes."

"Then fuck yes I want it."

She found herself smiling. "Heal up quickly. We have a lot of work to do." Amarante leaned down and pressed a soft kiss to his lips. "And I wouldn't want anyone else at my side but you."

EPILOGUE

TWO WEEKS LATER

*S*moke clogged the air, great plumes of it blackening the sky. Amarante had never seen anything more beautiful in her life. She lifted the last child into the truck and closed the door. A soft rumble and it headed down the road after the others, each driven by one of the Horsemen. She turned to look at the ruin that used to be Camp Bueller's replacement. They'd come in the night and slaughtered every single adult in the place. The thirty children there were in varying conditions. Hopefully, they'd be able to return as many as possible to loving homes. Time would tell.

"It's finished." Tristan had a streak of soot down the side of his face. "Or at least this part of it."

"Yes." Emotion rolled over her, heavier than anything she experienced while circling Zhao. This was what was important. The difference they'd made in these children's lives. There were other innocents being hurt by things he'd put into play, too many to count. This first step mattered, though. In some ways, it was the most important one.

Her phone vibrated, and she dug it out of her pocket. "Hello?"

"It's done." Cora sounded tired, more tired than she ever had before. "Chimera is dead."

The last of the tension left Amarante and she leaned against Tristan. "I'll settle the last half of the bill immediately."

Cora hesitated. "This was more complicated that we first expected. That's why it took so long." She cleared her throat. "I want a favor, Amarante. Open-ended. There may come a day when me or one of mine needs help, and I want you to give your word that you'll provide it."

She didn't even have to think about it. "Done." She would have agreed even without Cora removing the threat of assassination.

"Good." She sounded relieved. "That's good."

Amarante frowned. "Did something happen?"

"No, nothing like that. Nothing concrete. I just have a bad feeling."

Cora wasn't one to be dramatic. If she felt like something was barreling toward them, it likely was. "Keep me updated. You're always welcome on the island, of course."

"Thank, Amarante. I appreciate it." Voices in the background. She cleared her throat. "I have to go. Talk to you soon."

She hung up and slipped the phone back into her pocket. "We don't have to worry about assassins any longer."

"Today's turning into quite the day." Tristan slung an arm around her waist. "Let's get moving before Cami decides to start adopting orphans."

The thought sent a thrill of true fear through her. "She wouldn't."

"The woman has a heart of gold and baby fever that's strong enough to scare the shit out of me. She definitely would."

She picked up her pace, hurrying to the truck they'd parked off to the side of the road. "That's not funny."

"Who's joking?"

But when she looked at him, he was fighting down a grin. "You're such an asshole." She put the truck into gear and pulled out, going slightly faster than strictly necessary. Tristan might have been joking, but she'd seen the look on Cami's face when she'd gathered the smaller children up. The faster they could get those kids to safe places *away* from the Island of Ys, the better.

"You love it."

"I love you." She reached across the console and took his hand. "Let's finish this and go home. At least until the next one."

"Life with you is never boring. I wouldn't have it any other way."

* * *

THANK you so much for taking this journey with me to the Island of Ys! It's been a wild ride, and it's very bittersweet to have reached it's conclusion!

If you're craving something a little darker and a whole lot sexier, check out DESPERATE MEASURES! It's the first in a brand new series that reimagines fairy tales through the lens of the villain winning...and them being kinky AF!

Want to stay up to date on my new releases and get exclusive content, including short stories and cover reveals? Be sure to sign up for my newsletter!

Join my Patreon if you'd like to get early copies of my indie titles, as well as a unique short story every month featuring a couple that YOU get to vote on!

* * *

KEEP READING for a sneak peek of DESPERATE MEASURES!

"I'LL MAKE YOU A DEAL, JASMINE."

Another trap.

That's why my heartbeat kicks into high gear, a stampede of one in my chest. Fear. Understandable and justifiable, considering my circumstances. It's certainly not something akin to delight at the opportunity to pick up whatever gauntlet he's about to throw at my feet.

Jafar moves away, his features still hidden from me in the darkness. As if I don't have them memorized, from his close-cropped black curling hair, to his medium brown skin that darkens over the summer months, to his perfectly groomed beard. And those eyes. Those dark eyes *haunt* me.

He stops near my bed, and I would give a fortune to know his thoughts as he looks down at the tangled sheets where I spend every night. Finally, he turns to face me. "Run, Jasmine. If you make it to the front door, I'll release you, trust fund intact."

Run.

I plant my feet. "And if I don't?"

Another of those sinful chuckles. "Then you're mine, body and soul."

A thrill cascades through me, intense enough to steal my breath. *His.*

No. I give myself a shake. No, no, *no*.

I've fought a losing battle from the time I first realized my place in my father's business, fought to be considered an actual person instead of an asset. Since I realized that my body and looks are more important than anything my brain can accomplish. If my father truly is gone, that means I have a chance to set a new course.

But only if I make the right move tonight.

I part my lips, the word that would set me free tingling against my tongue. *Rajah*. That's what I should want, isn't it? To be gone from this place and this man and all the strings attached to what he's offering me. Just another kind of ownership.

You're mine, body and soul.

No misunderstanding his meaning.

If he catches me …

I shouldn't want him to catch me.

With a shaking breath, I put away my desires. They betray me the same way this man betrayed my father. Deserving or not, it *is* a betrayal. I pull my robe more firmly around me, a laughably worthless action considering how short and silky it is. The slick fabric reveals more than it conceals, and if I wonder if the shadows blind Jafar the same way they do to me, his nearly soundless inhale at my movement tells me—he can see me enough to want me.

But then, he's always watched me with a hot gaze beneath those hooded eyes.

And me? I enjoyed the attention. The thrill of it, of how forbidden it was to be desired by *this* man.

More the fool I was. He's just as bad as my father. Worse, in some ways, because while my father had many faults, breaking his word was never one of them. For better or worse, when he said he'd do a thing, he followed through on it.

Jafar promised my father his loyalty.

Look where that's left us.

I take a step back, and then another. A third brings me flush with the door. "I will walk out that door with my money *and* my freedom."

"Then run, Jasmine. I'm feeling generous, so I'll even give you to the count of ten."

Generous? Never. More like he wants to draw this out, to give me a moment where I can actually taste victory before he snatches it away. This is all a game to him. *Everything* seems to be a game to Jafar.

I don't hesitate this time. I throw open the door and flee down the hall, my bare feet slapping the cold tile in time with my racing heart. The front door never felt so far away. Three staircases, half a dozen halls, more rooms than I care to count. All of it stands between me and my freedom.

If you really wanted freedom, you should have used your safe word.

I ignore the sensible voice whispering through me. Freedom without resources is no freedom at all. This is the only way.

I reach the stairs as my bedroom door opens behind me. Even though I know better, I look over my shoulder as Jafar steps into the hall and adjusts the cuffs of his suit jacket. God, he's magnificent. Evil and manipulative, and far too attractive for my peace of mind. Our gazes collide over the distance and the slow curve of his lips into a satisfied grin nearly sends me falling down the stairs.

He starts toward me.

I flee for my life.

Pre-order DESPERATE MEASURES now!

ABOUT THE AUTHOR

New York Times and USA TODAY bestselling author Katee Robert learned to tell her stories at her grandpa's knee. Her 2015 title, The Marriage Contract, was a RITA finalist, and RT Book Reviews named it 'a compulsively readable book with just the right amount of suspense and tension." When not writing sexy contemporary and romantic suspense, she spends her time playing imaginary games with her children, driving her husband batty with what-if questions, and planning for the inevitable zombie apocalypse.

www.kateerobert.com

Keep up to date on all new release and sale info by joining Katee's NEWSLETTER!

Made in the USA
Columbia, SC
21 January 2025

52187791R00140